He sa_____ghtest
pair of Levi's _____

The heels of his suede cowboy boots clicked against the floor as he strode to the back of the convenience store.

The sight of a cowboy in Phoenix wasn't unusual, especially during rodeo week. This one simply packed a wallop. He was definitely hunk material.

At twenty-nine, Kelly Shelton thought she was past dreamy-eyed stares. Amused that she'd even noticed him, she pivoted back toward the snack cakes, her mouth watering in anticipation of those chocolate cupcakes with the gooey cream centers.

A package in hand, the cellophane crinkling beneath her fingers, she whirled toward the cashier.

And saw the gun pointed at her.

Dear Reader,

Well, it's that loving time of year again! Yes, it's February—and St. Valentine's Day is just around the corner. But every day is for lovers at Silhouette **Special Edition,** and we hope you enjoy this month's six novels dedicated to romance.

The February selection of our THAT SPECIAL WOMAN! promotion is *Sally Jane Got Married* by Celeste Hamilton. You met Sally Jane in Celeste's last Silhouette Special Edition novel, *Child of Dreams.* Well, Sally Jane is back, and a wedding is on her mind! Don't miss this warm, tender tale.

This month also brings more of your favorite authors: Lisa Jackson presents us with *He's My Soldier Boy,* the fourth tale in her MAVERICKS series, Tracy Sinclair has a sparkling tale of love in *Marry Me Kate,* and February also offers *When Stars Collide* by Patricia Coughlin, *Denver's Lady* by Jennifer Mikels and *With Baby in Mind* by Arlene James. A February bevy of beautiful stories!

At Silhouette **Special Edition,** we're dedicated to publishing the types of romances that you dream about—stories that delight as well as bring a tear to the eye. That's what Silhouette **Special Edition** is all about—special books by special authors for special readers.

I hope you enjoy this book, and all of the stories to come.

Sincerely,

Tara Gavin
Senior Editor

Please address questions and book requests to:
Reader Service
U.S.: P.O. Box 1325, Buffalo, NY 14269
Canadian: P.O. Box 1050, Niagara Falls, Ont. L2E 7G7

JENNIFER MIKELS

DENVER'S LADY

Silhouette®

SPECIAL EDITION®

Published by Silhouette Books

America's Publisher of Contemporary Romance

SILHOUETTE BOOKS

ISBN 0-373-09870-7

DENVER'S LADY

Copyright © 1994 by Suzanne Kuhlin

All rights reserved. Except for use in any review, the reproduction
or utilization of this work in whole or in part in any form by any
electronic, mechanical or other means, now known or hereafter
invented, including xerography, photocopying and recording, or in
any information storage or retrieval system, is forbidden without
the written permission of the editorial office, Silhouette Books,
300 East 42nd Street, New York, NY 10017 U.S.A.

All characters in this book have no existence outside the imagination of
the author and have no relation whatsoever to anyone bearing the same
name or names. They are not even distantly inspired by any individual
known or unknown to the author, and all incidents are pure invention.

This edition published by arrangement with Harlequin Enterprises B. V.

® and TM are trademarks of Harlequin Enterprises B. V., used under
license. Trademarks indicated with ® are registered in the United States
Patent and Trademark Office, the Canadian Trade Marks Office and in
other countries.

Printed in U.S.A.

JENNIFER MIKELS

started out an avid fan of historical novels, which eventually led her to contemporary romances, which in turn led her to try her hand at penning her own novels. She quickly found she preferred romance fiction with its happy endings to the technical writing she'd done for a public relations firm. Between writing and raising two boys, the Phoenix-based author has little time left for hobbies, though she does enjoy cross-country skiing and antique shopping with her husband.

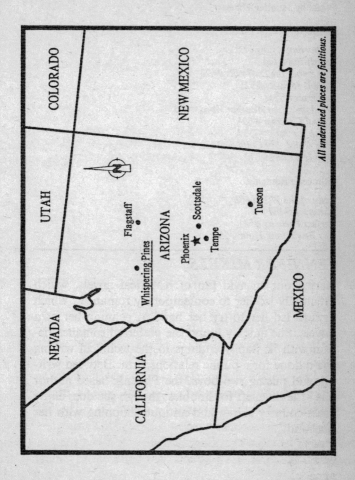

All underlined places are fictitious.

Chapter One

He sauntered in wearing the tightest pair of Levi's she'd ever seen. The heels of his suede cowboy boots clicked against the floor as he strode to the back of the convenience store toward the refrigerated cabinet. The sight of a cowboy in Phoenix wasn't unusual, especially during rodeo week, but this one packed a wallop.

Dark, shiny hair peeked out from under his hat. Cut long, the thick strands brushed the collar of his chambray shirt. She guessed he was in his early thirties. High cheekbones were strongly chiseled, and even though he wasn't smiling, faint lines marked the corners of his eyes. He was what her sister called "hunk material."

At twenty-nine, Kelly Shelton thought she was past the age of dreamy-eyed stares. Amused she'd even noticed him, she pivoted back toward the rack filled with snack cakes.

Some people craved steaks. Others drooled over whipped cream. She succumbed to those packaged chocolate cupcakes with the gooey creamy centers.

While she'd been driving back to the magazine after an interview, her mouth had watered in anticipation for one of those cupcakes. Weaknesses of any kind annoyed her, but she'd decided long ago that she'd sacrifice a size six for this one.

Behind her, the buzzer signaled the entrance of more customers. A package in her hand, she whirled around. The cellophane crinkled beneath her fingers as she stared at the two men now at the door, at the gun aimed at the cashier. Briefly she considered tossing her purse at the lankier man, a youth just out of his teens, who was snatching money from the cashier.

Heroics played well only in the mind, she reminded herself.

Kelly peeked at the cowboy. He appeared oblivious to what was happening at the door. The other customer, an elderly man, was bent over, his arthritic fingers curled around a can of peas. Through the thick lenses of his wire-rimmed glasses, he squinted at the label on the can.

While the younger robber shoved the money into a paper bag, his cohort waved his gun. "Don't try anything," he warned as if reading her mind.

The cashier shook his head.

Kelly tensed at the gun pointed at her.

"Don't plan to," the cowboy drawled, suddenly close behind her.

The youth with the bag scampered backward toward the gunman. He'd moved to stand outside the door, ready for their getaway.

Peripherally Kelly caught movement. The cowboy inched closer to her now. She didn't dare look up at him, but she felt the heat from his body as evidence of his closeness. The warm, firm pressure of his hand enveloped hers, then gently he tugged downward. She grasped his message. Duck.

An urge to hold tight, to keep him from doing what she'd silently wished for only seconds ago, rushed through her. As the youth with the bag turned to flee, the wondrous protector charged forward. Unbelievably agile, he hurtled the cupcake rack forward and slammed into the man's back. With a thud, they both hit the floor.

She'd seen less efficient tackles on television during Sunday-afternoon football games. Still, no match for the hero of the moment, the youth remained flattened to the floor.

Her mind in gear again, Kelly skirted a display of cookies and raced toward the door to catch a glimpse of the gunman's getaway car.

"Hey." The telephone receiver glued to his ear, the cashier snagged her arm before she could reach the doorway. "You can't leave," he shouted. "I need witnesses."

She jerked away from him. "I'm not leaving. Anyway, you have that." She pointed at the in-store surveillance camera aimed toward her.

"It isn't working."

From outside, she heard the squeal of tires and the blare of a horn as the robber cut into traffic.

Within minutes, sirens wailed. As lights flashed outside the store, uniformed officers ran in. One youthful-looking one whisked the handcuffed robber out the door while the older officer, a heavyset man with an overabundance of white hair, demanded their attention.

"We'll need statements from all of you." He flipped open his pocket-size notebook and nodded at his partner as the younger man came back in. "What did the one that got away look like?"

"Not too tall," Kelly said.

"Sure he was. And he had brown hair," the cashier countered.

Kelly shook her head. "His hair was blond."

The cop darted a look at the cowboy.

"Didn't see him that well," he said in a lazy, slow manner, as he casually leaned against the window of the store.

Feeling her credibility as an eyewitness deteriorating, Kelly added, "He was taller than average but—"

Pencil poised, the officer looked as if he longed to be anywhere but here. "Would you say he was as tall as him?" he asked, directing her attention to the cowboy.

Strolling away from the wall of windows, he moved with a casual, loose-limbed stride, yet managed to deliver the kind of confidence that would warn someone not to start trouble with him.

Closer to her, he tipped back his square-crowned beige Stetson, turned intense blue eyes on her and smiled. Damn, but he could buckle a woman's knees with that smile. She visualized him in full color on the cover of her aunt's magazine. You could be in pictures, she thought, nearly smiling herself. The cliché—tall, dark and handsome—fit him perfectly.

She felt a little jerk in the vicinity of her heart. The aftermath of too much adrenaline, she reasoned. A rational mind was her best trait as a magazine interviewer. Naturally she was unsettled. Hadn't she been staring down the barrel of a gun just a minute ago, her fate uncertain? Good solid logic explained away what another woman might assume was a physical reaction to this man. "A little shorter," she finally answered.

"Less than six feet?" The officer waited for a nod of confirmation from the cowboy about his height before scribbling in his notebook. "We'll need a better description of him."

"I can't help." The cowboy sounded apologetic. "I didn't see the other one. But he took off in a '91 Mustang."

"He what?" Kelly rushed to the window and sagged against the doorjamb. Dismally she stared at the vacant parking space. "That was my car."

"Left your car running?" the younger officer asked reproachfully.

She whipped around, not pleased about being chastised by someone almost a decade younger than her. "I only planned to be in here for a minute."

"I'll radio an A.P.B. on it," he said to his partner.

The older officer tucked the notebook back into his front shirt pocket. "In the meantime, we need all of you to come down to the station."

Witness three shuffled forward with his can of peas, his cane tapping on the tile floor. "How much are these?" he asked in a weak voice that began to tremble. His watery blue eyes took in the uniformed officers. "What's wrong? Have I done something wrong?"

Kelly brushed past one of the policeman and touched the elderly man's arm. "Everything is all right. You can go home." She glanced at the older officer for an agreeing nod.

He gave a cryptic laugh. "Sure, he can. Just give me your name," he said to the man. "Then, you can go."

Kelly, too, gave him her name and address. Wandering outside, she stared at the vacant parking space. She'd have to call her insurance agent. She'd have to file a stolen vehicle report. She'd have to sit for hours in a police station. And all she'd wanted was a cupcake.

"You look kind of pale." For the second time in minutes, the cowboy touched her. This time the pressure was lighter, warming the small of her back. "You sure you're all right?"

"Fine. I'm fine."

He offered a hand. "The name's—"

"William D. Casey. I heard you tell the policeman," she said absently, still thinking about the problem of her stolen car. As his hand remained open and extended to her, Kelly placed hers in his. The palm against hers wasn't smooth but ridged with calluses.

"Denver." He held her hand a second longer. "Everyone calls me Denver. And you're—"

Frowning, she looked down, aware her hand was still in his. "Kelly Shelton," she said, slipping it free.

"Kelly." His voice caressed her name as if stroking it for softness.

"You want to come with me, lady?" the older officer called out.

Kelly focused on the policeman and nodded. She was no fool. More than the robbery had disturbed her.

The squad room was hectic for a Thursday afternoon. At least half an hour passed before she was sitting at a detective's desk and reliving the robbery for him. He jotted down several notes, then dismissed her with a parting message to wait.

For the next ten minutes, she paced in front of the desk sergeant's counter. The station was a hive of activity. Two uniformed officers ushered a handcuffed man and a woman into the dismal rooms with their pea green walls. Another man complained to the desk sergeant about a neighbor's "junk heap" parked in front of his house. And a tourist in a flowery Hawaiian shirt asked for directions.

Impatient, Kelly glanced at the clock above the police station door. If the time was accurate, she was going to be late for a dinner date with Greg Kramer. At the moment, she was more concerned about her aunt. She'd have to phone her immediately. If she heard about the robbery from anyone else, she'd panic.

Hunting in her purse for coins, she ambled to one of two telephones near the exit. When the door opened to the detective's office, her hopes for a dismissal faded. Instead of the detective, the cowboy strolled toward her.

Denver sneaked another look at the blonde as he stood ready to make his phone call. Tall and slender, she was dressed in a peach-colored suit and a white silk blouse. She looked all business in a feminine way, and cool despite an unseasonably warm March day. She was the best thing he'd seen since arriving in Phoenix hours ago.

He watched her lips tightening, narrowing her full bottom lip and emphasizing the delicate structure of her features. He wanted to offer a soothing word. Where he was from, people drawn into a difficult moment banded together. Despite years of traveling from one city to the next, he still couldn't get the hang of city ways and the almost unspoken code: Don't talk to strangers. Under the circumstances, her coolness seemed kind of dumb to him. They were in a police station. He'd hardly be there if he was on this year's Most Wanted posters.

He plunked coins into the slot and punched out the number for his hotel room. Silently he cursed his decision to stop at that store. If he hadn't, he'd be at the rodeo fairgrounds now. But since his throat had been parched after driving through the desert, he'd needed something cool to soothe it. A beer would have suited him, but he'd been thinking about the competition and had mentally settled for a can of soda when he'd seen the kid stuffing the money into the bag.

Playing hero hadn't been his intention until he'd seen her frozen to the spot. He was a man who believed life crossed the good and bad in a person's life at the same time. If he'd skipped the rodeo, he'd have avoided the robbery, but he'd have also missed seeing her.

Uptight or not, she was the kind of woman a man dreamed about. He saw a romantic face, pale and delicate and sensuous. He'd read a poem about a woman who'd sprung from the sea, a woman with flowing golden hair and an enticing smile. Any sailor who saw her followed, mesmerized by her beauty. This woman had that kind of face.

Only inches from her, he smelled the scent of lemon in her hair. Because he was tempted to touch it, he jammed a hand into the pocket of his Levi's.

For no reason, Kelly reached up and ran a smoothing hand over her hair. She wasn't prone to imagining things, but she'd have sworn he'd touched it. "Aunt Jean, I'm running late," she said in response to her aunt's greeting.

"The interview was a good one?"

"Awful." Her feet still hurt from waiting overly long outside the basketball stadium for the interview, and her neck muscles burned from tilting her head back to stare up at the six-foot-nine star dunker for the Phoenix Suns. "He didn't want to discuss anything but his latest feats on the court."

"Then why are you running late?"

Kelly braced a shoulder against the wall. "I'm at a police station."

"You're where?" Her aunt's voice rose with concern.

"I'm all right," Kelly said to calm her.

Beside her, the cowboy was offering his own reassurances. "No, I wasn't picked up for speeding again. Jeez, Dooley, you're worse than a mother. If they gave out nagging awards, you'd win one. Yeah, I'm okay. But look, I'm not going to make it on time this afternoon. See what you can do about having me placed on a later schedule today."

"Kelly?" Her aunt grabbed her attention. "Why are you there?"

"There was a robbery."

"A robbery!"

At the anguish she heard, Kelly rushed her words. "I went to a convenience store and—"

Her aunt's more familiar tone returned. "Don't I always tell you to go grocery shopping weekly? If you didn't do a dash-and-run for junk food, you'd never go into places like that. You know they're easy targets for robbery."

"Yes, I know." Kelly had expected a maternal lecture about the virtues of broccoli and cauliflower over candy bars and cupcakes. "We'll discuss that later. Okay?" She laughed softly at the ridiculousness of the conversation. "In the meantime, I need you to call Greg. The police want statements from the witnesses, and I might not get home in time for our date. Would you call him for me?"

"You don't want to do that yourself?"

"He won't be home yet. He's still at the bank, and he doesn't like personal phone calls during business hours."

Her aunt sniffed disdainfully. "No exceptions?"

"No." Kelly moved the receiver to her other ear. A grand mistake. She stood so close to the cowboy that his spicy after-shave drifted to her. "Please call him and leave a message at his home phone."

"Was the last number five or nine?" her aunt asked at the numbers Kelly rattled off.

Kelly caught herself ogling a great set of male buns in snug-fitting Levi's. "Nine," she answered, facing the telephone once again.

"Will you call Jamie? Your sister might be upset if she hears about this on the news."

"It's a small convenience store robbery. I don't expect it to be newsworthy enough, but yes, I'll call her tonight."

"And me when you get home," her aunt insisted.

Kelly gave her a daughterly reassurance that she'd be the first one she'd call, then set the receiver back in its cradle.

Beside her, the cowboy propped a shoulder against the wall. "Quite a day."

A lazy jolt hit her again in the way of a slow and pleasurable spine-tingling sensation. She returned a stiff shrug, but it seemed like an unappreciative response to a man who'd played rescuer. "Did you get hurt?"

"I had a cushion." Humor edged his voice. "Him."

Kelly zipped up her shoulder bag. If she were interviewing this man, she'd describe him as unflappable.

"Seems we're going to be here a while longer." He gestured toward the vending machines. "Want a cup of coffee?"

A candy bar with almonds waved at her. "A candy bar." She noticed his veiled grin. "I can't believe this happened," she said, sharing the one recurring thought she'd had for the past hour.

"Life in the big city."

His voice carried enough disdain for her to guess he was one country boy who wasn't impressed with city living. "It has its advantages."

"Like?"

From the corner of her eye, she saw him check out her bare ring finger. "The symphony, theaters, art galleries."

He noticed green specks in her dark eyes. He was noticing a lot about her. "If you say so."

Kelly inched her fingers to the bottom of her purse in search of a quarter.

"Which candy bar?"

She broke away from her search in her purse to look at the display. "The one with almonds." Again, she pointed her face downward.

Smiling at her serious expression, Denver dropped the coins into the slot and pulled at one of the knobs on the vending machine. "Is there someone who might worry if he heard about the robbery on the news later?"

"My aunt." Frowning, she plucked out some coins nestled between her wallet and checkbook.

"Here."

As he held out a candy bar to her, she let the retrieved money slip from her fingers back into the bottom of her purse. "Thank you."

"What about a steady?"

She paused in tearing at the wrapper. "A steady?"

"Significant other or whatever?" he added.

Clearly he was making a move on her. It wasn't that she couldn't have been attracted to him. The man's looks had snared her attention the moment she'd seen him. Perhaps, because they did, she was even more guarded. "He might be concerned," she lied to simplify the moment.

"Guess he'll be upset that you're bowing out of tonight's date?"

She took a hearty bite of the candy. Eavesdropping obviously wasn't impolite in whatever godforsaken place he called home. Men she knew played more subtle, sophisticated games. Men who wore tailored suits. "He'll understand."

"Hey, folks," the desk sergeant called out. "You can go now. The detective will contact you if he has more questions."

With a glance at her wristwatch, Kelly sighed. Wasting time anywhere always frustrated her. She was a woman used to schedules.

"Guess we're sprung."

She nodded, eager to leave, but sounds behind them swung her around. She recognized several reporters and photographers from the local newspaper in the crowd gathering around the desk sergeant.

"Busy place."

"I wonder why," she said, puzzled. She'd been at the station for over an hour. If some newsbreaking event had occurred, she'd have been first on the scene. So why had the media arrived, looking hungry and eager? Curious, she dug her press badge out of her purse.

"You're a reporter?" A frown passed over his face so quickly that had she blinked she'd have missed it.

"I write for a magazine. *On the Town.*" Tense. He was tense suddenly. Reading people had become second nature to her because of her work. She took a moment longer to really study his face. She'd seen him somewhere. But where?

"What kind of magazine is that?"

Sidetracked as she tried to pin down why he looked familiar, she was slow in answering. "It's a monthly magazine about what's going on around town." She refrained from telling him that her aunt owned it. Learning that, people tended to underestimate her, believing nepotism was alive and well. But she'd worked hard to get a staff position, and her aunt was too much of a professional to expect less.

Denver allowed himself one last lengthy look at her. "See you."

At the softness in his voice, she shot a look up to see him sauntering toward the exit. Unless the police called them both in about the robbery, she didn't expect to see him ever again. Even if she were interested, she'd stopped liking chili and cowboy music years ago.

"Where is he?" she heard a reporter ask.

Curious, she sidled close to a photographer she'd met months ago. "Who's *he?* Why is everyone here?"

"There he is," someone else shouted, pointing.

"Mr. Casey!"

"Denver, wait."

Dumbfounded, Kelly watched the rush toward him. Denver Casey? She groaned aloud.

"I'll be," a uniformed officer murmured to the desk sergeant. "Hey, Mel, you had a celebrity here."

Kelly bolted for the door on the trail of the throng already filing onto the sidewalk.

Behind her, she heard the officer's words, "All-Around World Rodeo Champion. Past four years."

Outside, reporters trailed Denver and rattled questions. He outdistanced everyone to reach a run-down, white pickup truck.

If it were physically possible to kick herself, she would have at that moment. She'd just allowed an interview with the celebrity of the week to slip through her fingers. Every newspaper and magazine in Phoenix had some reporter trying to get an interview with Denver Casey.

"You aren't telling me that you were alone with him, that he was talking to you, that you had the chance to interview him and—"

"Blew it," Kelly finished for her aunt that evening. She dropped to the closest chair and tucked the telephone receiver between her jaw and shoulder while kicking off her shoes. Her feet still ached. And not recognizing Casey had bruised her professional pride. "I don't follow rodeo," she said. It was a good excuse but didn't make her feel less foolish. "Do you?" she asked, knowing her aunt didn't even like horse-back riding with her.

"No, of course, I don't."

"So how would *I* know him? Anyway, I wasn't thinking clearly after the robbery." Kelly wiggled her toes. "Did you call Greg?"

"He said as long as you couldn't make it on time tonight, he'd prefer to postpone your dinner date until another evening. Strange manner if you ask me. I told him what happened, and he wasn't the least concerned."

"Did you tell him I was all right?"

"Yes."

Kelly shuffled through her mail, then tossed it aside. "Then why would he be concerned?"

Her aunt snorted.

"We aren't anything but friends."

"Well, maybe you'll see him again."

"Greg?"

"Denver Casey. If you have to go to court, maybe you'll see him again."

Uncharacteristically, Kelly gnawed at a corner of her manicured thumbnail. "I probably will." She wasn't comfortable with the idea. Intelligence, even shrewd-ness lurked behind Casey's carefree manner, quick-forming smiles and country charm. Before knowing he was a rodeo star, she'd tagged him as a man's man. He had the rough, callused hands and lean athletic build of a man who strained muscles daily. And he had eyes that made a woman feel as if she were the only one in the world.

Chapter Two

The morning newspaper ran a story on page one about the robbery at the convenience store. The reporter praised Casey as a hero and included statistics about his rodeo career. Still peeved at herself, Kelly tossed the newspaper onto her sofa and rushed back into her bedroom. If he hadn't been at the store during the robbery, the story would have been tucked away on page twenty.

"Kelly?" Her sister's yell accompanied the slam of the front door. Wearing black leotards and an oversize shirt, her younger sister breezed in and plopped onto the unmade bed. "I saw this morning's newspaper," Jamie said without a greeting.

Kelly smoothed her panty hose over her thighs. "Don't you ring the doorbell anymore?"

"Oh, Kelly." That was the extent of any apology for barging into her sister's apartment.

Kelly slipped into her pumps. "What if someone was here?"

"Such as?" Jamie asked, as if the idea were ludicrous. She tossed back blond curly hair and twisted her legs to sit yoga-style. "You never have anyone sleeping over."

Kelly gave up subtly admonishing Jamie about invading her privacy. Nine years separated them. A youthful twenty, Jamie drifted from job to job, from boyfriend to boyfriend, from one cause or interest to another, blissful one moment and discontent the next.

Lately, she'd been going through some I'm-finding-myself phase that included lessons in everything from modern dance to cake decorating. She hadn't stayed with any of the lessons for more than two weeks.

"When you called last night, why didn't you tell me that you'd met Denver Casey?"

"I thought after my name was mentioned in the newscast about the robbery that your major concern would be with my safety," Kelly said meaningfully. "There was a gunman. Remember?"

Jamie's eyebrows veed. "Oh, I was concerned a little. But if something had happened to you, Aunt Jean would have told me."

Standing before the mirror, the brush in her hand, Kelly smiled at her sister's reflection. She looked so young. Was it immaturity that made her so dreamy? No, they were as different as night and day. Had Jamie been an eyewitness to a robbery, Kelly would have needed to hear her younger sister's voice for reassurance that she was safe. A big sister protective complex seemed an eternal part of her.

Jamie's voice softened with an apology. "I'm really sorry, Sis. I didn't mean that I wasn't glad to hear you were okay. But why didn't you tell me about *him?*" She joined Kelly at the mirror. "All day yesterday, I tried to get an introduction to him."

Puzzled, Kelly set down the brush. "Why?"

"Kelly, he's a star." She sounded baffled that Kelly didn't understand the obvious. Wrinkling her nose in disgust, she fingered her shoulder-length hair and tugged at a kinky curl, the result of a too-tight permanent that she voiced hating daily. "Do you think I should bleach my hair?"

"Why would you want to?" Kelly sidestepped her to grab a cream-colored silk blouse from the closet. "Have you thought about what I asked you?"

For a long second, Jamie stared dumbly at her. "Oh, you mean about moving into that house with you?"

"We never had a house when we were growing up. Aren't you sick of apartment living? As long as there isn't anyone special in your life right now, when I get the house, you could move in with me."

"I don't know." She made a face. "I'm not crazy about mowing lawns."

Kelly gave up with a sigh. She was actually looking forward to homeowner tasks. All she had to do now was hope her realtor's persuasive powers worked on the stubborn seller who seemed adamant about not lowering his asking price.

"And there is someone special now."

Because there hadn't been yesterday, Kelly came to full alert.

"I was disappointed that I didn't meet Denver, but I did meet someone."

Kelly could recall half a dozen men her sister had been infatuated with during the past year. "Where did you meet him? At the rodeo?"

"No. Until finals, it's boring. Who wants to watch a loser?"

"Back up," Kelly insisted. "Who is this guy?"

"A friend and I went to the rodeo fairgrounds. We learned everyone was going to this Western dance hall—Cowpunchers."

"Cowpunchers?"

"That's the name of it." She tugged again at a kinky strand. "So we went there. He's a musician, a guitarist," she rambled brightly. "And right from the moment I walked in, he was watching me. Later, he came over to where I was sitting with some friends. Johnny. Johnny Bellows. He's really nice. You'd like him."

Kelly thought a reminder was necessary. "He'll be here today and gone tomorrow. Why get involved with him?"

"Oh, Kel, you miss out on so much fun because you're always thinking about tomorrow."

Kelly refrained from reminding her that last year she'd idolized some guitarist with long purple hair who wore a snow-tire chain for a belt. "I want to talk more about this." She swept a look at her alarm clock. "But I have to run. Are you free this evening?"

"Not tonight." Jamie bounded from the bed. "I have a parapsychology class tonight."

"Tomorrow then."

"Oh, sure." Halfway to the door, she breezily waved goodbye.

Kelly fiddled with a gold earring and worried.

Denver yawned for the third time since he'd arrived at the fairgrounds. Though it wasn't yet eight in the morning, a bright sun blazed against his back. A foam cup in his hand, he ambled past participants pinning number cards to their backs. A sassy-looking brunette in a brand-new Stetson flirted, tossing out an innuendo that held a promise if he was interested. He wasn't.

For some reason that was driving him loco, he couldn't get the image of a tall, cool blonde in a peach-colored suit out of his mind. He didn't like any woman bothering him that much and screwing up his concentration. Women waltzed in and out of his life. Being on the rodeo circuit, he'd never started a serious relationship. How could he? The next town had meant new faces. For the past ten years, that had suited him fine.

"Heard you played hero yesterday." Calvin Pringle, Denver's biggest competitor, twisted a corner of his dark handlebar mustache and smirked.

Denver prepared himself for some good-natured gibes.

Cal's brother-in-law, a sandy-haired calf roper, joined in. "The Lone Ranger rides again."

Denver laughed. "Some of those calves you bring down give more of a fight."

Cal guffawed, seeming satisfied Denver had kept his ego down. "You gonna give us some excitement this year, too, Denver? Last year, I thought for sure you weren't gonna get free of that stirrup."

Longingly, Denver eyed the cigarette Cal had lit. "Nearly busted my leg."

"If you had, I'd be wearin' that buckle." Cal motioned with his head at the World Champion buckle on Denver's belt. "If not this year, then next year, Denver."

Denver nodded and grinned, but he wasn't sure he'd be around to win this year's belt. Too many broken bones could leave a man useless for ranching. As far as he was concerned, there was nothing else. Ranching was all he'd ever wanted, but at one time, he'd needed to satisfy a curiosity, sample a different world.

Meet different women, he reflected. A smile touched his lips as he thought of Kelly Shelton again. She had style. She also understood about working hard, he mused, remembering how tightly her fingers had clutched her purse during the robbery.

"Sit down. You're making me nervous," Dooley grumbled, squinting up at him. A friend and companion on the road while they'd traveled the rodeo circuit, Dooley participated only in calf roping. Seated against a corral that blocked the spectators from the livestock, he taped a wrist that had gotten caught in a rope during a bronc ride seven years ago and had never stopped aching.

Denver hunkered down beside him and squinted at the sun. "What was your time in the preliminaries?"

"Third fastest. Cal's baby brother isn't going to beat me this year. I'm winning the calf-roping event."

Denver sat down, stretched his legs and crossed them at the ankles. For a few minutes, he sipped the muddy-looking coffee and listened to Dooley's comments about the women passing by, but he paid little attention.

By the time a man reached thirty-three, he learned a lot of small lessons and few big ones. One of the big ones in his life focused on staying with his own kind. For sure, Kelly Shelton wasn't one of them.

City oozed from her. He was used to a different type, women in Levi's, who liked horses and country music and didn't think about anything but the moment.

But what man wouldn't have taken a second look at that face?

She was intelligent, too. That was something he respected. He hated air heads, women who couldn't form a sensible thought.

Then there was the old kick in the gut to deal with. Though he wasn't susceptible to a woman's wiles, he wasn't a man to ignore the sexual pull when he felt it. There might be the clue, he decided. She practiced no feminine tricks; she'd done nothing to attract him, yet here he was thinking about her like a moonstruck sixteen-year-old.

She'd told him she had a steady. He'd bet the championship buckle on his belt that she'd lied. So that didn't count.

How she made her living was another matter. When he took a woman out, he didn't want her dissecting his every word. But all his life, he'd faced adversity head-on. Now wasn't any different. He'd enjoy going one-on-one with her, watching how she'd manipulate conversation.

He drained the coffee in his cup. Stubbornness had always been a guiding force in his life. One bull had dumped him six times before he'd successfully ridden him. The defeats had only made Denver more determined. Simple logic had led him. He couldn't stop challenging that damn bull until he'd been the winner. The same kind of reasoning existed now. To get her out of his mind, he had to see her again. "Let's go."

At Denver's nudging elbow, Dooley raised his head lazily and scowled at him. "Go where?"

"On the town."

The day wasn't going well. Her insurance company wouldn't pay for the rental car. Accompanying photographs for one of her stories couldn't be found, and a computer glitch wiped out two weeks of notes. Kelly realized just how off kilter the day was when Greg called.

With no more than a brief hello, he went on quickly as if pressed for time. "I have a party to attend on Saturday. I'll pick you up at eight."

Perhaps it was a cranky mood or too many problems—like a sister overly influenced by a stranger or a certain cowboy who'd invaded Kelly's thoughts too often already today. Whatever the reason, she resisted what sounded like an order. "I'm busy," she said though she had nothing planned. "You could have asked sooner—"

"You could change your plans," he cut in.

"No, I couldn't do that."

He was silent for a long moment, then gave her a goodbye as clipped as his hello had been.

Kelly set the receiver back in its cradle. Maybe she'd overreacted, but she was tiring of their relationship. Though she dated Greg casually, he'd become more possessive lately, demanding. The notion of belonging to some man, being controlled by him filled her with panic.

If a woman got too caught up in a man's life, she'd end up with none of her own. Once she'd thought she'd found the love of her life. But Kevin had taught her well. She knew now that total love for another person was simply self-destructive.

No, she wanted no personal turmoil. She'd spent years climbing the ladder to succeed. Some people viewed her as remote, unapproachable, ambitious. Other descriptions pleased her more—accurate, concise, hardworking. She had goals. One of them was in reach.

After years of working, she could afford the house of her dreams. She could have purchased one sooner, but she'd been waiting. Now, she'd found the perfect house. With luck and an agreeable seller, she'd be in it within months.

Denver led the way into the marble lobby of the high rise. "There's the directory."

Behind him, Dooley grumbled. "What are we doing here?"

"I told you already." Denver scanned the directory for the floor that the magazine's offices were on. "Seeing a lady." Last night, he'd had the hotel clerk send up any copies he could find of *On the Town*. While Dooley and friends had been out enjoying some of the nightlife in Phoenix, Denver had spent the evening in his hotel room reading interviews written by Kelly Shelton. She was good. She nailed strengths and weaknesses. She explored until secrets were revealed. That didn't worry him. He'd let her ask questions. In the end, he'd learn more about her.

"Seems to me we should forget about this."

Denver focused on the directory again. "What's the problem?"

"Why is it when you see a stop sign, you keep right on going?"

Ignoring him, Denver strolled to the elevator and jabbed a finger at the elevator button. "What stop sign?"

"Look around you. We don't belong here," he said, frowning at two men in expensive-looking suits strolling into the high-class lobby.

"Just because you can't smell hay, doesn't mean you can't be here."

"Sure we can be here. But we don't belong here. And whoever she is, she does."

"So?"

"So, I'd think you'd already know that. You're supposed to learn lessons from your daddy."

"I'm not marrying her." Denver stepped ahead of him into the elevator. "I just want to see her."

Kelly paced her aunt's office silently while her aunt talked on the phone. The room was simply decorated in a Southwestern tan and pale blue decor, with Indian art. On the desk were photographs of her and Jamie. Kelly eyed her own youthful image. Gangly, her hair flying, her grin impish, she was riding a horse. Her tomboy years belonged to another lifetime, another world, one she'd outgrown at nine. Reality had whisked away childish notions.

She'd been the big sister, the one to care for Jamie while her stepfather was away. Still mourning her mother, she'd just finished feeding Jamie when the men had come up to the house. Even before she'd opened the door, she'd known something terrible had happened. As best as they could, they told her something about a rigging, had spoken the words she'd known before they'd been said. She hadn't cried. She'd been too numb.

She hadn't known what to do. Alone with a baby, she'd been frightened. Even more frightened when the dark car had pulled up in front of the house. She'd clutched Jamie, certain they'd come to take her. They'd come to take both of them.

Wards of the state. The words still made her cringe two decades later. With a sigh, she abandoned the memory and listened to the end of her aunt's conversation. In her late fifties, Jean Moore was a sophisticated woman with gray hair softly framing her face in a short, turned-under style. While she charmed an advertiser who'd been planning to drop his advertisement in the magazine, Kelly was reminded of the magazine's financial woes.

Personable yet firm, her aunt was convincing the caller to stay with them another few months. Letting out a long breath, she set down the telephone receiver. "Well, they'll stay with us for a while, but if our circulation keeps dropping, we may lose everything. I can't blame advertisers. Subscriptions are down." She leaned back in her chair and peered over the ornate, silver rims of her glasses. "Now tell me. What is it about Jamie's new boyfriend that worries you so much?"

"I don't even know him, but she's so impressionable, so easily caught up in her infatuations."

"She is young."

"Not that young."

"No, you're just old," her aunt teased. "At fifteen, you were going on thirty. So serious."

Kelly smiled with her, able to laugh at herself. She knew she'd always been too serious. She set goals, she believed in schedules, she led a cautious, well-thought-out life. "What if Jamie gets too involved with this man?" she asked, perching on the corner of her aunt's desk.

"Kelly, she's had her share of infatuations before."

"This one might be more serious."

Her aunt inclined her head. "Why would you think that?"

"Cowboys have some romantic myth attached to them. They're different from the men she's known."

"He's not a cowboy, is he?" She shuffled papers on her desk and lifted a sports magazine to the top of the stack. "He's a musician."

"Yes, he is, but..." On the cover of the magazine was a photograph of Denver. His hat tipped back to a cocky angle, his blue eyes sparkling with devilment, his smile seeming almost familiar to her now. She released the breath she'd been holding and wondered how many women had bought that issue of the sports magazine just for that cover.

"She has to make her own mistakes, Kelly," her aunt said in a soft manner. At Kelly's silence, Jean looked up quizzically at her.

Kelly pushed away from her aunt's desk. "I know," she answered, unsettled that something as simple as a photograph had stirred a flutter inside her. "But she might make a big one this time."

"Wait and see." Jean ended her deciphering stare and slid off her suit jacket. "I'm more concerned about you since you told me you could identify that gunman," she said while she draped her jacket over the chair.

"So can three—make that two—other people." She doubted the elderly man would do well identifying someone in a lineup when it took him minutes to read a simple label on a can.

"Denver Casey is one of those people?"

Her back to her aunt, Kelly concentrated on a painting of an adobe village. "Well, no, he said he hadn't seen him."

"So only the cashier and you can identify him?"

Kelly swung around. "Aunt Jean, what is this all about?"

"Your sister's little flirtations aren't important. What I'm concerned about is your problem. The danger to you."

"Danger?"

"You're an eyewitness to an armed robbery. You did say that the one man had a gun."

Kelly rounded the desk and touched her aunt's shoulder. "Don't you have enough trouble already?"

"I'll always worry about you. But yes, I do seem to have more than usual." She removed her glasses and rubbed the bridge of her nose. "Obviously, many publications are having similar problems, but..." Jean tapped a finger at the cover of the magazine before her. "That face on the cover of *On the Town* might help us."

"He's known for being media shy," Kelly reminded her.

"A shame."

Though Kelly saw merit in her aunt's idea, she didn't relish spending days at the rodeo trying to inveigle information out of a man who made her nervous whenever his eyes met hers.

With the magazine rolled in her hand, she strolled out of her aunt's office and stopped at the vending machine for coffee.

Head bent, watching the steaming brew in her cup, she passed rows of desks. Briefly she stopped to make small talk with one of the copy editors. "How was your daughter's birthday party?"

"A blast. Thanks for the name of the clown. Where did you hear about him?"

"I used to work with him years ago. We were both stuffing chicken wings into buckets in those days."

"I had a job like that, too, once," she admitted laughingly.

From across the room, a thin brunette, festooned with necklaces of cameras, rushed toward her. "I found those photographs," she said, a touch winded. The magazine's photographer, she was a little scattered but a near genius with a camera. "Sorry about that."

"It's okay, Steph." Kelly smiled. "I'm glad you found them."

"I don't know where . . ." She cut her words short, her dark eyes widening. "Oh, he could wash my back any day," she practically purred.

Smiling at her comment, Kelly swiveled a look over her shoulder to see who had distracted her. Around her in the large room, heads turned and voices buzzed with whispered questions, following the two men as they walked down the long aisle. While the shorter man's stride hesitated as if he wished he were somewhere else, Denver moved purposefully in one direction—toward her.

"God, he's gorgeous," Steph murmured, viewing him with narrowed eyes as if looking through her camera lens. "I wonder who he's here to see."

Me, Kelly guessed, forcing herself forward to meet him. "Good morning."

Despite the polite smile, he heard an edge of annoyance in her voice. It wasn't the mood Denver had hoped for. But for now, he decided, any emotion was better than indifference. "'Morning."

He stepped closer, enough to make her nervous. "Why didn't you tell me who you were?"

He knew exactly why he hadn't. It had been a nice change to be with someone who hadn't recognized him. "Why don't we start over?"

A little uneasy, she tightened her grip on the magazine. "Start over?"

His smile widened, cutting dimpled grooves in his face. "Are you free for dinner?"

Kelly's immediate response was to say no. She didn't like having the fluttery feelings of a teenager for any man. But all it took was a glance away at her aunt's office door to change her mind. "That would depend on whether or not I can bring my tape recorder along."

He was going to enjoy himself more than he thought. "Meet me for lunch without it, and I'll let you know."

One time might be enough. She was trained to coax information out of people. For her aunt, for an interview, she'd be a fool not to accept an hour alone with him to pick his brain. That his looks were distracting was something she'd have to bypass. "All right. Lunch." She studied him a moment longer. She never liked being made to look a fool. "You'll get a chance to meet my aunt," she added to inform him ahead of time this was strictly business.

"Just say where."

She rattled off an address, doubting he'd be smiling when he saw where she'd told him to meet her. She couldn't help still wanting to find a subtle way to even the score. "You, too, Mr...." She made eye contact with his companion.

A gaunt-looking man with a weathered face, he gave her a wary grin while nervously moving the brim of his hat between his fingers. "Just Dooley, ma'am."

"Join us," she said brightly, then looked down before her smile gave her away.

At ten minutes after twelve, Kelly saved a story on her computer, then fingered the magazine her aunt had given her. He looked like a movie version of the archetypal Old West hero. The flattering photograph captured the sheen of his dark hair, the penetrating deep-set blue eyes and the dazzling smile that belonged in a toothpaste commercial. In the flesh, he was even more intimidating.

Because it was her habit before talking to celebrities, she'd done some homework on him. The four-page spread about him in the sports magazine had focused more on the rodeos and quotes from other participants. While she'd skimmed the article, she'd seen three different photographs of him, including one in which he was hanging on to the reins of a flying bronco, but it didn't feature one quote about his personal life.

She had the facts now about his rodeo career, and from a copy of his birth certificate, she'd learned that he'd been born at a Flagstaff hospital to William Casey and Mary Ellen Grener. In a matter of time, she'd find out why Denver Casey insisted on such privacy.

Taking one of those deep breaths that experts claimed were calming, she snatched up her shoulder bag from under her desk. Second thoughts made her grab the magazine to take with her.

Stepping outside, she squinted against the bright sun in a cloudless blue sky and reached in her purse for sunglasses. A warm, late-March breeze swaying palm fronds tossed at her hair. She brushed back some wayward strands and hurried her pace toward her aunt's favorite restaurant, an elegant tearoom in a first-class hotel. It epitomized elegance with its sweeping staircase and marble floors. The restaurant's style was impeccable, its service formal to a fault. Anticipating Chef Lamont's specialty, baked sole filled with crabmeat, Kelly rushed to the door, wondering if Denver was already there.

She entered the restaurant, a little smile of anticipation curling her lips. She couldn't think of anything more incongruous than a cowboy sitting in a ladies' tearoom.

Chapter Three

Gutless Dooley had bowed out the moment the maître d' had muttered something sounding French.

Denver wondered why he hadn't scooted off, too.

He'd watched the stiff-backed man's nose raise as if he'd sniffed something foul before he'd gestured toward a table reserved for Mademoiselle Shelton.

Seated on a chair meant to be a perch for a smaller backside, Denver looked away from the rose-colored tablecloth. He viewed the chandelier overhead and stared past the embossed wallpapered walls to the marble fountain. Around him were mostly women dressed in clothes designed, no doubt, by people with foreign names. The few men seated at tables wore suits. Nothing in the room appeared to have been made in the good old U.S.A.

Shifting, he damned his long legs and tried to get comfortable. He'd been bamboozled. He'd allowed her smile to sucker him in. Feeling about as comfortable as a cowboy stuck in patent leather shoes, he shifted again on the chair. He longed for the sound of a boot spur. He yearned to be in a saddle. He wanted to be anywhere else, even facing a stampede of mustang.

That didn't mean he wouldn't make the best of an uncomfortable moment. Being flexible was a necessity on the road. Too often during the early years, he'd slept sitting up in his pickup and had eaten nothing but cheese and crackers. When success had come his way, the homes of the upper crust had opened to him. He could handle an hour in some snooty restaurant.

What he wouldn't treat lightly was dealing with her. He knew he was taking a chance. She wrote for a living. In the past, he'd dodged the media, allowing speculation but carefully guarding his private life. A smart reporter could learn statistics about his rodeo achievements but little else. He sensed she was smarter than most.

Steps from the table, Kelly saw his cocky "gotcha" grin. He looked outlandish sitting on a delicate mauve-colored chair with his denim-clad legs stretched out under the table and a striped tie, obviously supplied by the maître d', hanging lopsided and loose at the opened collar of his blue chambray shirt. Unfamiliar with his surroundings, uncomfortable and definitely out of place, he should have been at a distinct disadvantage, but he looked amazingly relaxed. "Mr. Casey."

Standing, he grinned slowly. "Ms. Shelton," he answered, wondering how long they'd go on pretending this was strictly business.

"Where's your friend?"

He tilted his head as she sat down and her hair caught the lights of the chandelier. "He took one step in and left."

So they'd be alone until her aunt arrived. She could manage a few minutes alone with him. *Forget the way he looks at you and think business,* she railed at herself. "My aunt is usually punctual."

"That's all right. I have plenty of time." He felt an urge to trace the faint line between her eyebrows with his fingertips. "Want to wait for her or order now?"

"Order," she answered. She could care less whether they ate or not. What she didn't want was to be alone with him too long. He emanated a masculinity that made every feminine instinct inside her spring to attention.

With another shift on the small chair, Denver cast a sweeping glance around the formal restaurant with its tuxedo-clad waiters, then opened the menu. He had a taste for a hamburger. Skimming over the French words, he spotted the only one he knew, escargot. If snails were the best that the restaurant could do, he was going to starve. "Is this good?" he asked, hunching closer and pointing to some indecipherable words on the menu.

Kelly looked up slowly. He'd scooted closer, his face inches from hers. "Boneless chicken in a mushroom sauce. It's excellent."

Around them, people were watching, and for good reason. In this restaurant, no one snuggled. Ladies shared tea, men chatted about business, but no one ever carried on a midday tryst in the bright room with its oh-so-proper ambience.

He grimaced slightly. "No steaks?"

"No steaks." Hiding a smile, she retrieved her pen and a small notebook from her purse. She could already jot one comment. He was a good sport. Actually, she'd gathered more of an impression of him. Laid-back, easygoing, a man who didn't get ruffled easily or lose his temper quickly.

Being observant, noticing nuances when interviewing people, was part of her job. As he hunched forward, setting muscular forearms on the table, hands that she already knew felt strong and callused didn't fiddle with silverware. In fact, she caught no telltale signs of nervousness in him. She couldn't say the same for herself. "I'm sure you know that my magazine would like to do an interview with you."

He waited until the waiter was done hovering around them. "I don't give them." With his palm, he nudged aside the bud vase with the single rose that was blocking his view of her. "Do you like roses?"

Glancing at the notes she'd taken about his rodeo background, she answered absently, "They wilt."

"Most women like them."

It took a moment for her to realize he was still discussing flowers. "Most women are romantics."

"You aren't?"

She met blue eyes that a woman could get lost in. "Not at all."

She intrigued him, Denver realized. It was that simple. She looked crisp and cool and all business, yet he kept wondering what she'd look like riding a horse or running barefoot through a meadow of daisies.

"There are things you could tell that would offer encouragement to other rodeo participants," she said, rushing into business quicker than usual. "You're a four-time winner of a rodeo buckle. People want to know about you."

She'd made the comment as if the buckle was unimportant. He'd battled for that damn buckle. Anyone in rodeo knew the hardships involved if they wanted to win one—too much traveling from one rodeo to the next, missed meals, lack of sleep and too many bruises and broken bones.

As she flipped open the magazine to the article that concerned him, Denver eyed his own image grinning back at him. He didn't like seeing the photograph in the magazine. It was a candid shot that someone had sneakily taken when he was talking to friends. It was a look meant for people he cared about. But the two other photographs were less personal—and less flattering. In one photograph, he stood at a corral surrounded by women. In the other, he appeared to be kissing a rodeo queen whose name he couldn't remember. Only he knew that *she* was kissing him.

"It says in here that you're from a small town in northern Arizona." Kelly stared at the chicken set before her and wondered when she'd forgotten she wanted the impeccably prepared baked sole. "When you were young, was being a world champion your goal?"

Having been cornered often enough by others in the press, Denver knew exactly what she was doing. He sensed a strong will, a competitiveness, an assertiveness that he usually didn't find particularly feminine. But he couldn't forget the softness he'd seen in her eyes when she'd mentioned her aunt, or the sensitivity he'd witnessed for a bewildered old man with a can of peas. "Tell me about yourself first."

She looked up with a frown. "My request for an interview has little to do with me. I want this interview for my aunt." That was the truth. She'd do anything for her. "We need something solid or *On The Town* might be out of business soon," she said honestly.

His resistance softened. Until now, he'd thought ambition was motivating her. "What does that have to do with me?"

"*Sports Today* proved you have screen-idol appeal. Their sales skyrocketed with the last issue because you were on the cover."

In his opinion, good genes had a lot to do with that. Reaching for his water glass, he gave a short laugh. "Looks mean nothing."

If he was playing the role of modest for her benefit, he was good at it, Kelly mused. "It does when an unending list of accomplishments goes with it. You work in what is viewed as one of the last truly macho occupations. Men carrying briefcases have secret fantasies about doing what you do. And women..." Kelly shrugged a shoulder. "I'm sure there are always plenty of them hanging around."

"So I'm a marketable commodity?"

She raised her head slowly. "You understand business?"

"My major in college."

It took willpower not to let her eagerness show, but she was aware no one had ever printed anything about his schooling. "When did you get a degree?"

He smelled her perfume, a springtime scent that made him think of wildflowers. "I'm no Joe College," he said with a laugh. "It took time in between rodeos, but I managed to earn a degree after eight years."

A tinge of admiration crept through her personal resistance to him.

Denver studied her for a long moment. She'd be a difficult woman to get to know. He thought that might be an impression she'd worked hard to convey. "How long have you been with the magazine?"

"Three years." Kelly forced herself to meet his stare over the rim of her coffee cup. "Before that, I worked my way through college doing odd jobs."

"And then?" he asked, watching the way strands of her hair brushed her cheek with the movement of her head.

"I assure you I'm a professional." She could see why he was a winner. He was a watcher, a man who probably spent hours eyeing the animal he'd ride, gauging its strengths and weaknesses. "I spent time playing gofer at a Los Angeles newspaper before joining a small Tucson one." She set down her cup. "I wrote obituaries, and feature stories about prize-winning roses. Only after proving myself did I join the staff at my aunt's magazine.''

She ate another forkful of chicken, then edged her plate aside. ''During your sixteen years on the rodeo circuit, you've given few interviews. By being mysterious, you fuel interest.''

''Mysterious?'' He released a soft laugh. ''That's a new description.'' He watched sunlight from a nearby window play across her face. Too tempted not to, he toyed with a strand of her hair. From the moment they'd met, he'd wanted to touch it. Silk couldn't be softer, he thought as he caressed one of the sunshiny strands. ''Do you always come to places like this?''

Deliberately she waited until she was sure the quickening of her pulse had slowed down. ''You don't like it here?''

Amused at her haughty tone, he asked, ''Don't you know of some place for dinner where they serve steak?''

The eyes holding hers made her slow to answer. They were sitting in a brightly lit restaurant, yet every time he looked at her, she felt the seduction of moonlight drifting over her. ''Not really.''

''If you did, would you go with me?''

''No.''

He let the strand slip through his fingers even as he yearned to bury his hand in her hair. ''Why not?''

He looked so puzzled. She fought a laugh, certain it would only encourage him. ''This wouldn't work for either of us.''

''You're going to explain, aren't you?''

"I'd think it was obvious. You don't want to give an interview, and I don't see any other meeting ground. We're two people from two different worlds."

She'd made everything sound so cut-and-dried. If that were true, why did he feel a tug at his insides whenever he was around her?

"We have nothing in common," she said simply.

"You're so sure of that?"

She was sure of only one thing. He could sweep her off her feet if she wasn't careful. Romance wasn't something she wanted in her life. The last time she'd given in to it, she'd been hurt. And she'd learned to be sensible, learned that women who let emotions lead them, lost. Not for the first time, she nervously glanced toward the entrance, not as much to watch for her aunt but to escape his gaze. Whether it was sparkling with humor or darkening with seduction, it unsettled her.

"You remind me of a horse I once had," he said in a casual tone that veiled his thoughts. An insidious attraction existed. Though he hardly knew her, in the short time he'd been with her, he'd already sensed he could burn for her.

She swung a look back at him. In her whole life, she'd never been compared to a horse.

"She was a spirited beauty. And skittish."

"And?" she asked, waiting for the proverbial next shoe to drop.

He watched a touch of humor tug at the corners of her lips. "And some need more time spent with them," he answered.

"In other words, she required patience."

His gaze didn't waver. "And soft words. Gentle hands."

Disturbingly she felt warm from his silly conversation. She had the distinct impression that he was giving her a warning of what to expect from him. As he signaled the waiter, Kelly stirred herself. "I invited you," she said, trying to reestablish a business mood.

He didn't cooperate. Standing, he took his wallet from his back pocket. "Where I come from, men pay."

With another man, she might have protested. But in the short time she'd been with him, she'd gathered impressions. One of them clearly declared that this wasn't a man who changed his mind easily.

Turning, he casually strolled away without another word. She laid a hand against her chest as if to will her heart to slow down. If he'd agreed to the interview, she might be worried, but he'd refused. There would be no reason to see him again. Slowly she released the breath she hadn't realized she'd been holding.

Around her, people were staring, some smiling. Kelly looked over her shoulder to see if he was gone. Inwardly, she groaned. He stood at the maître d's desk, his large hand curled firmly around her aunt's.

Nothing had gone as she'd planned. He'd been stingy with answers. He'd also made her uneasy.

"Well, now," her aunt murmured seconds later. She settled on the chair Denver had vacated. "That was surprising. I never expected to see Denver Casey here. Did you talk to him?" Her aunt nodded a thank you to the waiter for bringing her usual cup of tea.

"I had lunch with him—*alone.*"

"Sorry I was late, dear... but I did meet your cowboy, and though I spent only a few moments with him, he seemed far more charming than George."

And frustrating. She'd had lunch with him and had been fed mere tidbits of information. "Gregory," she said in response to her aunt's statement.

"Gregory," her aunt parroted with a touch of disdain.

Kelly smiled at her. "How can such an intelligent women forget his name so often?"

"By choice. He's dull. On the other hand, Mr. Casey is rather electrifying." Jean peered over her cup at Kelly. "He bothers you," she said with the sixth sense of a mother.

"He surprises me too much." Kelly finished her coffee. "Why were you late?"

"I stopped to see Jamie. You were right. She's acting very bewitched. It must be the boots. Or the hats."

Or a soft voice. A glint of humor in his eyes. The way his smile makes a woman forget what she wanted to say. "I don't know why Jamie's attracted to her country-and-western musician, but I've never known a man who complimented a woman and a horse in the same breath."

"He did?" Laughter softened her aunt's voice. "That must have sounded so much more genuine than the lines you're used to hearing." She stirred sugar into her tea. "An interview with him—"

Kelly raised a halting hand. "Forget it." She doubted anyone would be successful getting an interview with him. He had a knack for turning conversation away from himself. That in itself was a rarity in someone accustomed to being the center of attention. "He refused."

"Did he?" Her aunt smiled in an odd way. "Well, he gave me these."

Kelly stared in disbelief at the tickets for the rodeo.

"One for tomorrow. And two for the final day." Jean slanted a look at her. "I don't think we should refuse. I for one have never been to a rodeo."

"You could live your whole life and never attend one and not miss it," Kelly reminded her.

"But you'll go, too?" her aunt questioned.

Kelly shrugged noncommittally.

"I suggest you do since he's agreed to an interview."

To say she wasn't surprised would have been a lie. "When?"

"Just now." Her aunt peered over her glasses at Kelly. "Strange, isn't it? He claims that he doesn't like interviews, never gives them, which means he keeps his distance from the media. Yet, he came to our office, insisted on lunch with you, gave us these tickets. And now this? Why do you think he changed his mind?"

She'd been with him enough to believe he rarely changed his mind. "What difference does it make? Who are you sending?"

"Why, you, of course. That was the one stipulation. He'll give the interview only to you."

She'd underestimated him. Recalling her own words, she realized he was providing them with the one thing she'd declared was their only meeting ground.

"Why don't you tell me what's happening?" Her aunt settled back in her chair, assuring Kelly she would wait for an explanation.

"Nothing."

"Except we have a little more leverage than other people have, don't we?"

Kelly gave a sigh. "My job is all that matters to me. You know that."

"Yes, I do." Sadness clouded her aunt's eyes. "And I curse Kevin every day for making you feel that way."

Her aunt was wrong to blame him for anything. Kevin had only taught her a lesson she should have learned years before.

"Do you want me to tell him we've changed our minds?"

Weariness settled over her suddenly. In the past, she'd have jumped at a chance for this kind of interview. She'd worked hard, too hard to let one man make her forget professional responsibility. "No, I'll do it."

Affection warmed her aunt's eyes. "You never have let me down."

How like her aunt to forget what Kelly would never wipe from her memory? Without her aunt, she and her sister would have lived for years shuttled from one foster home to another. They'd have had nothing.

"It'll be interesting to see what you can learn."

Hadn't she already learned enough? From the first moment she'd seen him, he'd excited her. Excitement wasn't something she expected from a man. She looked for reliable, companionable men, and relationships that never demanded more than she was willing to give. Until this morning's phone call, Greg had suited her. Now, she had doubts.

Remembering that she was supposed to meet him Friday night at the art gallery, she considered not going just to avoid another unsettling moment. After all, it wasn't a date. An arrangement. He dated others, and she ... well, she liked her life uncomplicated.

Trying to get it back on an even keel, she returned to her office. She shoved papers aside and stared at the rodeo tickets. A day at the rodeo didn't thrill her. But she'd go for a little while tomorrow and watch him show off, then leave a message to set up an interview time in her office. It wasn't her usual way, but with him, nothing had been usual so far.

Feeling more in control of her life, she renewed her concentration on the story she'd started earlier. By four, satisfied with it, she clicked off the computer.

Snatching up her purse to leave, she hesitated as the phone rang. She nearly ignored it, but ringing phones were like a magnet to her.

An unfamiliar masculine voice answered her. "Ms. Shelton." He identified himself as the detective she'd talked to on the day of the robbery. "We wanted to keep you informed. We found your car. It's been totally stripped."

In disbelief, she sagged back in her chair. Her stomach churned while she listened to the rest of his news.

He wouldn't think about her. That had been Denver's plan while in a chute with a black mustang that afternoon. But while soaking sore muscles in bathwater before dinner, he wondered if her aloofness was enticing him. During his youth, he'd spent a lot of time sitting on a horse and rounding up cattle. Left with only his own thoughts for company, he knew himself well. He'd never enjoyed anything that came too easily.

By the time he joined Dooley in the hotel dining room for dinner, he still didn't have any answers. "Think I'm crazy, don't you?" he asked.

Dooley shoveled in a heaping forkful of mashed potatoes. "If you got to ask, you must think you are," he mumbled. "Thinking about her is okay. What you're going to do is what's bothering me."

Him, too. She sure wasn't like any other woman he'd ever been interested in. She was more like his mother, a woman with exquisite skin, stunning beauty, sophisticated tastes. A woman too soft for a country boy.

He returned to his hotel room, opening the door to the sound of the ringing phone. In passing, he flicked on the television, picked up the receiver, then offered a greeting to the caller.

"Seemed to me you should be going to bed by now. It's nearly eleven. At home, you got to go to bed early to get up early. Did you already forget?"

Denver grinned at the familiar sound of his father's gruff voice. "I haven't forgotten, Pa." He couldn't recall his father ever sleeping past eight in the morning, even when sick. "Why did you call?"

"To wish you luck. I won't be around a phone. That prize mare of yours had a filly."

"You need a portable phone," he said, aware of how his father would react.

"Phones don't belong in barns," he answered predictably. "Isn't it enough I let you talk me into that dang computer? Why, I don't know. Only you know how to operate it. It's just sitting there, collecting dust."

"I guess I'll have to come home and clean it off."

"Sounds like a smart idea to me. Anyway, don't break your neck before you get home."

"I don't plan to. I'll see you next Sunday."

"Looking forward to having you home, son."

Home. Denver set down the receiver, then fell back on the bed and stared at the blank ceiling in the unfamiliar room. How many years had he been at this? Years of highways, motel rooms, strange surroundings. He longed to see the ranch again, his father, people who'd known him from the time he was born. For months, he'd been looking forward to the trip home. But the anticipation was duller, that desire shaded by thoughts of a woman.

He didn't believe in love at first sight. He wasn't even sure he believed in love. He did understand passion and his own longings. With something as simple as a smile, she'd sparked desire within him.

He was only beginning, he realized. She was a different kind of challenge. He wasn't seeking any trophy, any champion status. Something was driving him. He couldn't put a name to the emotion, but while stuck in the city, he wouldn't willingly walk away from this woman.

Chapter Four

Sunshine glared against the chrome of pickup trucks and cars in the huge parking lot outside the fairgrounds. Kelly wished she'd changed clothes, including shoes. With each step she took, dust coated the tips of her black pumps. She was going to look ridiculous in her gray suit and pale turquoise silk blouse against everyone else in jeans, cowboy boots and hats. When she'd left the office, she hadn't stopped to consider her attire. She had a ticket for the day's two o'clock performance, a promise from Denver for an interview and an uncharacteristically vicious hope she'd watch some bucking horse throw him to his backside, bruising it but damaging nothing else.

She handed in her ticket and passed through the gate. It occurred to her as she scanned the crowd that he might be difficult to find. She was mistaken. She turned around and found herself looking directly into his eyes.

Leaning against a corral post only feet away from her, he was listening to a pert brunette who possessed a winsome smile and a propensity for touching.

Kelly felt a quick unexpected flutter and more. As he raised a hand and tipped back his hat, as his stare lingered on her, disturbingly she felt heat. Before, she'd ignored it. Now, it sizzled between them.

"Glad you decided to accept my offer." He stifled a grin at her mildly disinterested look in the direction of the livestock. Whatever her feelings were about the rodeo, he'd never doubted she'd come.

"You dangled an irresistible carrot in front of me," she said far calmer than she felt.

Looking over her shoulder, the brunette didn't even blink at being replaced. "I've got to fly. But before I go, did Cal give you my chili recipe?"

"I'd have beaten him bloody for it." Denver handed Sally the number card he'd picked up for her husband. "Don't forget this."

She laughed. "I almost did. Guess my husband's forgetfulness is rubbing off on me." She cast Kelly a smile, then scurried away to join her friends.

Kelly met Denver halfway. "My aunt said that you've agreed to an interview. When's a good time?"

The all-business tone nettled him, but he quelled his annoyance as swiftly as it had formed. For a little while, he'd play this her way. "Now is fine."

"Now? Aren't you participating?" She'd assumed he'd be pinning a number on his back, anxiously waiting his turn.

"Not today."

There went her theory about his inviting her so she could see him doing his macho thing. "First, I want to be sure I understand," she said so seriously that he couldn't help but smile. She noticed and ignored it. "You're willing to talk to me now and answer questions?"

Denver nodded, wondering if arrogance would be his downfall, but what could she learn in a week? Nothing he wanted to keep private. "I don't have a problem with that."

Kelly couldn't get a handle on him. Why would a man who'd avoided interviews agree to one? "So you'll answer my questions?"

"Most of them."

She touched her shoulder bag, itching to take out the pen and notebook inside it. "But not all?"

"Would you?"

Her fingers tightened on her purse strap. "I don't have anything to hide."

"I wonder. Isn't there a part of yourself you'd want to keep private? A love that disappointed you? A childhood dream that faded?"

Sensing a door opening, Kelly rushed in. "What childhood dream faded for you?"

"I am what I wanted to be."

"Seriously?"

"Seriously." Peripherally he caught movement and looked down. Decked out in jeans and boots and a wide-brimmed black hat that was too big for him, a boy about nine gave him a large-toothed grin. Denver took the paper and pen from him and scrawled his signature.

The kid's smile widened. "Thanks."

"The future of rodeo," he quipped, watching the kid race away and feeling suddenly old.

Kelly gestured with her head toward the boy. "Did you see the makings of a rodeo champion in him?"

He answered her smile and cupped her arm to steer her away from the crowd. "All it takes is determination and a willingness to get a few bruises."

She noted a competitor was taking a bouncing ride on a horse. She thought it probably took a lot more than that. "So you always wanted to be a rodeo champion?"

"I wanted to be a rancher."

Looking down at the souvenir brochure she'd got at the gate, she hid a smile. She wondered if he realized how much he'd revealed. While they walked, she fanned pages of the brochure past credits, honoring the organizers of the rodeo, the queen and her court, the announcer, the clowns. Head bent, she flipped to the two pages filled with photographs of him. "It says here—"

"Read about the rodeo clowns," he cut in. Without missing a step, he closed the book in her hands. "You should interview one of them. They'd make a great story."

With the experience she'd gained through the years, she discerned he would, too. She suppressed an eagerness to dig below the surface, certain now that he'd require time to open up to her. "Are you being evasive or modest?" she asked lightly about his suggestion.

He chuckled. "I've been called a lot of things, but never modest."

Nearing his truck, she chose a personal question he'd have no reason to resist. "Why the name Denver?"

"It was the first place that I won a rodeo."

She nodded as she recalled information she'd read about him. "A junior rodeo."

He stared at her dust-coated heels. "So you've done some research."

"You had the most points ever accumulated by a junior contestant. But that's just stats. You're a million-dollar cowboy. You've qualified for the National Finals Rodeo ten times, claimed four world titles."

The way she'd rattled off the statistics about him, she made everything sound so easy. It hadn't been. "I entered over a hundred rodeos a year to do that."

"That's a lot of traveling."

"An understatement." He paused to watch her withdraw a pocket-size notebook from her purse. "Want me to repeat everything?" he teased.

She leaned back against his truck and scribbled quickly. "Go on."

So serious, Denver mused. "I traveled thirty-five thousand miles last year."

"Did you always do that much traveling?"

"No." He inclined his head. She'd jotted down notes in a neat, precise handwriting. "How about a pizza?"

She looked up from her notes.

"We won't call it a date."

Mentally she added two more descriptions about him. Stubborn and persistent. "I like pepperoni."

Sitting in a corner booth of a ma-and-pa pizza parlor, Denver resigned himself to more questions as she took out her notebook.

"You were talking about the traveling," she said with a glance at her notes.

He accepted that he'd have to give her some information. This was safe ground. "When I was younger, I traveled less. After I'd been in junior rodeo for a while, I decided to try to make a living on my own away from the ranch, see the sights, spread my wings, whatever you want to call it." He took a swig of the beer set before him. "I hit every small-town rodeo there was across the United States." His lips curved in a self-deprecating grin. "And lost most of them."

The pen in her hand stilled. "How old were you?"

"Seventeen. I was always broke and starving. Then I lucked in. I hitched up with the meanest bronc alive."

What he considered "lucking in" amazed her.

"And rode him," he said, looking amused. "I didn't have much more money in my pocket, but I had respect. So when I traveled, old-timers began giving me hints, taking me under their wings. And I began to learn. There's more to rodeoing than just climbing on top of a broncing horse and riding him. There's a way to ride him," he said somewhat distractedly with a glance at the jukebox in a corner of the restaurant. "Got a favorite song?"

"You pick it." She watched him draw a few female stares as he sauntered to the jukebox. She couldn't understand anyone willingly preferring to lead a gypsy life-style. He'd moved around constantly; he called no place home.

A soft mellow song filled the room about a fickle-hearted lover. She ignored the salad just set before her. "What did your family think about your competing?"

Denver cradled a slice of pizza on his fingertips. "I lead my own life."

As honest as the answer probably was, Kelly had had enough questions dodged by the best to spot evasiveness. An off-limits sign flashed in front of her. For the moment, she took their conversation down a different path. "During those lean years, did you ever want to give up?"

He stared at her bent head, at the strands of blond glistening beneath the sunlight spiking through a nearby venetian blind. "I never give up until I get what I want."

She looked up, drawn not by his words but the softness that suddenly had edged his voice. If only he'd stop looking at her as if she were the only woman around. "So you wanted the title?"

"Everyone who competes wants it," he said between bites of the pizza.

"But you got it."

"A competitor needs to be a positive thinker." Denver settled back in his chair. "Anyone who rides a bull better be."

A game had begun. She wanted details; he offered generalities. Kelly dropped the pen in her purse and ate her salad. She had days now to learn about this man. Experience had taught her the importance of timing. "When will you give me more time?"

As she looked up at him with questioning eyes, he caught another whiff of the fragrance clinging to her. Desire kept crowding him. He wondered what he was doing with her when half a dozen more agreeable women haunted the lobby of the hotel for him. "Whenever you want."

"Tomorrow?"

He leaned across the table and brushed his mouth across hers. "Tomorrow."

He was good as his word. The next afternoon, Kelly trailed him around the rodeo grounds. She hadn't forgotten the caress of his mouth. Or the veiled promise in his voice. Whether she wanted him to or not, he was going to kiss her, really kiss her before this was over. She couldn't recall feeling so unnerved since she was fifteen and had been anticipating her first kiss after a school dance.

She sighed heavily, annoyed at the way her feelings and thoughts kept seesawing about him. It wasn't as if she'd never dealt with an attractive man before.

With a glance at her watch, she strolled toward Denver's truck to wait for him. She studied her notes. She had the statistics, Denver's thoughts about rodeo, friends' comments. One of the cowboys had told her frankly that Denver was too tall, too big to be as good of a bull rider as he was. Bull riders were usually short, wiry men. But Denver was one of the best.

All of that was ordinary information that had been duplicated in a hundred other articles about him. She shook her head, wondering if she was losing her touch. During other interviews, she could turn a corner and find someone who didn't like the celebrity she was interviewing. She couldn't say the same this time. While the competition was fierce among the contestants, the camaraderie overshadowed it. They liked each other, taking time to offer help with taping ribs or lending a glove or cuing each other about the weak points of the animal they'd drawn. Most of all, she learned that they liked Denver.

So she was beginning to understand him. Yet she didn't.

There was a sensitivity behind the macho image. She'd been with him when he'd taken a side trip to an ice cream parlor to buy a pint of peach ice cream for a competitor's daughter because he knew it was her favorite. And she'd been near when he'd spent hours sitting with a retired rodeo cowboy who'd never made it big. With respect, he'd listened to the man tell about the good old days.

She'd have used that contrast in her article about him, even been pleased to have it except it affected her personally. How could she write that he always touched her arm when crossing a street? Or that his voice softened to a whisper when he wanted to be alone with her?

Denver threaded his way through the usual amount of buckle bunnies who flocked daily around him and anyone else who wasn't losing, and stopped for a soda.

"We're going for a beer," someone called out to him. "Coming?"

"I'll pass." He heard snickers behind him. He didn't give a damn. He wiped the back of his hand across his sweaty forehead and walked with one destination in mind. She was leaning against the door of his pickup truck. Wearing designer jeans and a blue T-shirt and silver earrings that looked like miniature boomerangs, she tossed back her head as the wind played havoc with her hair, then glanced at her watch, showing an impatience he was becoming accustomed to. "You're sunburned."

Lost in her thoughts, Kelly nearly dropped the can in her hand. "Are you done for today?"

"That's it until tomorrow."

She looked down to shove her notebook in her purse. "So you can leave?"

His hand stilled hers. He shifted just enough to keep her back against the truck. "One more thing."

Her heart quickening, even before he lowered his head, Kelly placed a hand to his chest to push him away. But she didn't. As his mouth closed over hers, her hand went limp. She felt the strength in his hand on her face, holding it still. She felt his heart's quick beat beneath her fingers on his chest. She smelled the masculinity of him with each breath she drew. But it was his mouth, firm and soft, moving over hers that captured all her senses.

She'd thought a kiss might stop her from wasting more time wondering about a moment like this one. But the mouth on hers was warm and firm and more persuasive than she'd imagined. In seconds, he made her want something she'd given little thought to in a long time.

Confusion and sensation mingled. Something began to stir inside her. She wasn't sure what, as slowly he drew back.

His eyes never leaving hers, he spoke calmly. "I've been waiting for that."

"Denver, we—"

With a fingertip to her lips, he silenced her. "Shh. It's only starting," he said softly.

"No." She drew the first deep breath she could since his mouth had met hers. "We're together because of my job and yours."

He smiled, looking amused. "Our meeting ground?"

"Yes."

His smile deepened. If warmth had rippled through him so quickly, then she wasn't as calm as she pretended. "What did you write?" Curiously he fingered the notepad sticking out of her purse. That she didn't resist his curious touch on it urged him to slip it out and flip it open to the first page. It all looked like chicken scratch to him. "What is this?"

She watched his hands, strong hands. "Shorthand."

"Doesn't seem fair that you can read it and I can't."

"Yes, it is. You might get a big head otherwise."

He handed the notepad back to her. "So you wrote nice things about me."

"Who said?" she bantered, almost clinging to the humor to avoid thinking about what had just happened.

A dimple cut into his cheek. "You said."

She looked down to hide a smile. "You always twist words to suit you. Do you know that?"

He laughed. "You like it. It makes you think harder."

It was a little unnerving how right he was. Had he been easier to understand, she wouldn't have been so interested. Despite a hectic life-style, he possessed a kind of tranquillity. There was a sense of self about him as if he took none of his celebrity status too seriously. She wondered where and when he'd found such peace within himself. And envied him for it.

She was always discontent with her work, demanding more from herself. She'd never been sure if it was to get ahead or to keep from sliding backward. She assumed it was a built-in fear that if she wasn't always alert and on guard, she might find herself at her beginnings, might fall prey to some man's charms and let him take over her life. So always she pushed herself, determined to be independent, to live her own life.

"Hey, Denver." A wiry man wearing a dusty-looking black cowboy hat stepped away from three other participants and gleamed his front gold tooth at Denver. "I heard Bigsby wasn't on the circuit at all this year. That true?"

Denver nodded, slipping a proprietorial hand around Kelly's arm.

Younger, with a flirtatious gleam in his eyes, one of the man's companions who was spiffed up in a turquoise shirt with an overabundance of studs, winked at Kelly before airing his opinion. "Bigsby's got more than a healthy fear that he'll get hung up in a stirrup again."

"'Cause he's out of shape," the other commented.

Kelly shot a glance at the arena. A horse exploded out of a chute and tossed its rider to the ground. "What happened to Bigsby?" she asked when the men stepped away.

"He shouldn't compete anymore."

Kelly craned her neck to see if the man thrown was limping.

"A horse fell on him." As she turned a look of incredulity on him, he shrugged. "It happens."

"It's happened to you?"

"Accidents happen." He slid a hand over hers. "There's always that chance."

"Often?"

A wry grin curled a corner of his mouth. "Which time do you want to know about? The broken leg, the cracked ribs, the torn cartilage?"

She gave him a thoughtful look, then realized he was serious. "Never mind."

Briefly he smiled. "It's a hazard of rodeoing." He raised his face toward the sun. "So is missing meals. Do you cook?"

Kelly looked up from the hand clutching hers, wondering when he'd taken it. "Cook?" She rarely cooked. She'd spent more time than she wanted to re-member cooking meals, cleaning the house and wash-ing clothes after school while classmates had been out playing. When she'd moved in with her aunt, she'd been stunned to learn that someone else would cook for her. "I hardly ever cook."

"How about doing it for a change? A can of soup. A sandwich?"

She laughed. "Why?"

"It's been a long time since I sat in a kitchen."

Against her better judgment, she agreed. She stepped ahead of him into her apartment, reasoning that she'd have more time alone with him than any re-porter ever had. That was good. And bad, she de-cided as he brushed her cheek with the back of his hand in passing. It wasn't that she couldn't handle him. She'd managed to keep at bay a film Casanova who thought the interview should take place in bed. The problem wasn't Denver, but herself.

Frustrated, she swung away and hit the button on her answering machine. All she had to do was re-member why she was with him, she thought, feeling a touch panicky as he ambled at a leisurely pace to her refrigerator as if he belonged in her apartment.

"You weren't kidding, were you?" he said with a laugh while skimming the sparse contents in her re-frigerator. "There's not much here."

"That's it."

Over the top of the refrigerator door, Denver noted the frown creeping across her face as she listened to an airy feminine message.

"Hi, Kelly. Jamie. I need to talk to you tomorrow."

"Trouble?" he asked when she joined him in the kitchen.

"My sister."

Moving to stand behind her, he surveyed the cupboard she was looking in. It was bare except for two cans of soup and a box of crackers. He took the can from her and flipped it around to read the label. "Vegetable beef? That'll do." He skirted around her to reopen the refrigerator door. "And I see a couple of eggs. Got any bread?"

Kelly sagged against the cupboards. It was getting more difficult not to admit one thing. She liked him. "Check the freezer."

"I'll make the fried egg sandwiches. You can set the table."

"I thought I was supposed to cook."

"Changed my mind." He hunched down and hunted for a frying pan. "Tell me about your sister," he prodded gently. "She's not like you?"

"Oh, no." She released a short laugh while opening the soup. "Not at all. I've always needed to know where I'm going. We don't understand each other anymore."

Head bent, he cracked eggs into the frying pan. They sizzled while she told him more about her sister and Johnny Bellows. He'd seen his share of women who'd do anything to be noticed by celebrities.

Kelly gathered plates and set them near him. "Have you heard of him?"

He dodged the question. "He's a musician. I'm rodeo. Not the same crowd." He gestured toward the bread. "We need toast."

"But you've heard of Cowpunchers."

"Is that where he plays?"

Her back to him, she nodded while she measured coffee grounds into the basket of the brewer.

"You want an honest answer?"

Kelly looked back, impressed by his skill in the kitchen. With a swift turn of his wrist, he flipped the eggs in the air. "Yes, I do."

He set the pan back on the burner. "If I had a sister, I wouldn't want her going there alone." At her silence, he stretched back to see a frown settling on her face. "You're close, aren't you?"

"We always were." She plugged in the brewer and turned to watch him slide the eggs onto the toast she'd made.

"Do you have any family except your aunt and sister?"

"No, I lost them long ago." She joined him at the table, setting down the soup bowls.

Denver wanted to know more but didn't want to hit a raw spot. "Your aunt told me you horseback ride."

Kelly handed him a napkin. "When?"

"When I told her I was agreeing to the interview. She wanted to assure me that you liked horses."

She wondered what else her aunt had told him. "Have you talked to her often?"

"Only a few times." Denver stretched out his legs under the table. "When did you learn to ride one?"

"When I was six." Cautiously she spooned the steaming soup into her mouth before answering, "My stepfather took me to a nearby ranch."

He fixed an intense stare on her. "You lived in the country?"

She heard the surprise in his voice and smiled. "It was the only life I knew as a child."

Interested, he set down his spoon. "You're not a city girl?"

She laughed. "I was born here. My mother came from a family of doctors, was supposed to follow in their footsteps, but after my father died, she met a man. Instead of finishing medical school, she went with him."

He kept probing, aware she was dropping her guard. "And lived in the country?"

"Yes." At ease, she stopped eating the soup to get coffee for both of them. "My stepfather was a wild-catter. I don't recall a lot of the early years, but we were never anywhere long enough for my mother to pursue her career."

Her mother had had nothing, Kelly recalled with almost agonizing clarity. Love had stolen her identity, made her forget her own dreams.

Denver waited for her to sit down again. He was beginning to understand her almost obsessive dedication to her work. "Tough life?"

Aware of his eyes intent on her, she managed to keep a frown at bay. "There were difficult moments. Like when she died."

He waited only a moment. "What happened?" he asked, sensing the more he knew, the better he'd understand her.

Kelly reached for her coffee cup. Her world had fallen apart. "She died in childbirth with Jamie. The weather was bad."

Two sentences cued him in. He grasped now what wasn't being said. In some ways, he represented a life that had left her with difficult memories.

"She couldn't get to the hospital," Kelly went on. "And my stepfather was out on a job, working at some place miles from us."

Denver thought of his own father. Will had suffered through a different kind of grief. It was something they'd shared for months. "What did you feel about him?" Through the turmoil in his own life, he'd become closer to his father. "Did you like him?"

It was an unexpected question, one she'd never considered before, maybe because she had cared for the gentle, smiling man who loved to sing. "He had a wonderful voice," she said with affection. "Whenever we were driving, he'd sing the whole time." She met Denver's stare. "Yes, I liked him."

Because the smile she gave him was weak, he gauged his words carefully. "And you miss him?"

She nodded. "Both of them. Ray died in a work accident the same year as my mother," she said simply. The grief had settled long ago, but the memory of that time seemed a breath away. "Authorities tried to notify my aunt, but they couldn't find her. She was living out of the country."

"I don't understand." He gave her his full attention. "Didn't you know where she was?"

Kelly shook her head. "My mother had broken off all relations with her family after she married Ray. My aunt didn't even know my mother had died or that Jamie existed until she returned to the States and was contacted."

Despite everything Denver had gone through, he'd never felt alone. "How old were you when you went to live with your aunt?" he asked, getting a clearer picture of why she had such an independent streak.

"Eleven."

An image of her, young and fragile looking, flashed in his mind. He noticed a flicker of sadness in her eyes as if she was caught up in a memory. "Were you scared when you came here to live with your aunt?"

Slowly, Kelly turned her head to him, stunned by his sensitivity. With incredible accuracy, he'd zeroed in on her emotions that day. How could he have guessed?

"Were you?"

"Petrified," she admitted softly. "I didn't know my aunt." She set aside her empty soup bowl. "I had my sister's hand in mine and prayed she'd like us. She met us at the train station. We were barely off the train when her arms were around both of us."

He grinned with her. "Special lady."

"Oh, yes." From the day she and Jamie had moved in with their aunt, she'd been Kelly's role model. At fifteen, she'd viewed her aunt as everything she'd longed to be—cosmopolitan, successful and independent. Meeting his gaze, she wondered with amusement who was interviewing whom. "You're a good listener."

He grinned. "Thank you."

That she'd told him so much surprised her. She'd been dating Greg on and off for six months and had never mentioned her past. "And a decent cook," she added, munching on her sandwich.

Denver responded to the teasing smile in her eyes. "Macho men cook these days." He looked toward the archway, wondering what the rest of her apartment was like. Her kitchen resembled a dozen he'd seen at home in ranch houses. It was a crisp white kitchen splashed subtly with color from the wallpaper to the place mats with their small blue flowers. Adorning a wall were blue-and-white dishes. Everywhere were baskets with dried flowers, and on the counter was a double-wheel coffee grinder, one similar to the antique at the ranch that his grandmother had had. A contradiction. The sleek professional was hiding a woman with homespun country tastes.

"I am impressed," Kelly admitted.

The spoon in his hand stopped in midair. "I don't believe it," he said on a laugh.

"What's funny?"

"That I managed to impress you."

She slanted a look at him. "I've always been impressed."

He warmed more from her impish grin than her words. "But wary," he said between bites of the sandwich.

At his sudden seriousness, she looked up.

"And resisting."

"Sensible," she countered.

Behind her, the phone rang.

Grateful at the interruption, she whirled around to answer it, hoping to hear Jamie's voice.

Silence answered her quick hello. When even heavy breathing failed to follow, she uttered another, "Hello."

Still no one responded.

Chapter Five

Suddenly she felt an eerie chill rush over her. She rarely watched horror movies alone because of an overactive imagination. Being unnerved by a prankster's phone call or wrong number seemed just as dumb. Frowning, she set down the receiver. "Why can't people at least say a simple sorry?"

Denver braced a shoulder against the refrigerator. She seemed tenser than she should have been about a silent caller. "Something happened that you're nervous about?"

She cursed her own skittishness. She'd lived alone too long to let a few phone calls unnerve her. She'd received prank calls before. It was nothing more, she reasoned. "Nothing happened." The lie slammed back at her as the phone rang again. Edgy now, she jumped and snatched up the receiver. Once more, she received silence.

"Why don't you tell me what's bothering you?" Nerves. He sensed them in her. "Does it have anything to do with the robbery?"

The earlier phone call from the detective still weighed heavily on her. Not wanting to worry her aunt, she'd said nothing to her about it. But he was sort of an interested party. "The police called me. The man arrested, George Evans, won't tell who his partner was. They believe, though, that the gunman was his older brother, Marvin. According to the detective, he has a long rap sheet and was just released from prison a month ago."

More than her words, the worry that briefly slipped into her voice alerted him. "And?"

"One of their witnesses backed out."

"It wasn't me. But then I couldn't identify the gunman. Who? The cashier," he said with disgust.

She nodded. "He suddenly can't remember what the gunman looks like."

With his shoulder, he pushed away from the refrigerator. "Why did the cashier back out?"

Her stomach knotted as she recalled the detective's words. "His tires were slashed, so he's scared now. Even if they pick up Marvin Evans, the brother, they have only—"

"One witness," he finished for her. "You." With her nod, he looked away, mumbling an earthy expletive.

Chilled though the night was warm, she grappled to steady herself. If she thought too much about what the detective had said, she'd be looking over her shoulder every minute. "So for safety's sake, I check my tires now," she said on a tight smile.

He gave her credit for not losing a sense of humor despite being obviously scared. "Did you ask for protection?"

"From what?"

He laughed mirthlessly. "From what?" He shook his head. "You're too intelligent to ask such a dumb question."

"I'm not going to be spooked by a few phone calls."

She was puzzling. She looked like a romantic vision from a nineteenth century novel but wore independence like a badge. It wasn't often that a man could find a soft-looking woman with a good mind and a pioneer spirit. Hell, he'd dreamed of finding one like that and thought he never would. "You should tell the police about the phone calls."

"I'll think about it." At his silence, she looked up. She'd nearly forgotten the words said before the phone had rung. One look in his eyes, and she knew he hadn't. Unsettled, she started back toward the sink, but he crowded her, placing a palm on the counter close to her hip. As his knuckles brushed her cheek, she drew a slow, steadying breath.

With an ease that amazed her, he leaned close enough not to touch her but enough to make her sway back against the counter. "Where were we before the phone call?" Possessively he skimmed her neck with a fingertip. "Oh, yeah." He laughed as she tensed beneath his hand. "Resisting."

"I meant what I said—"

He kissed her, silencing her before she could marshal her defenses. "My turn. What I can't figure out is why." That wasn't entirely true. In a way, he understood now that she viewed his world as one that could be harsh, too harsh. But was that really why she kept pulling back from him? "The way I see it, we get along pretty good. We have laughs," he reminded her. "We don't sit around staring at each other like we haven't anything to say. A minor explosion during a kiss suggests something worth bothering with. So why? Why don't you want to be with me?"

Kelly drew a shaky breath. "I told you why." Exasperated, she rattled off her reasons. "We have nothing in common. We live different life-styles. You make me feel too much...." Her voice trailed off. Stunned, she turned a confused look up at him, not believing she'd let those words slip out. Her heart hammering, she made an appeal. "I wish you would forget I said that."

He gave her a slow smile. "No way."

Curling a hand around the back of her neck, he skimmed his lips over her jaw. She braced herself, but even before his mouth slanted across hers, she was imagining his taste. With a will of its own, her body leaned into the heat of his. He murmured something. She didn't care what he'd said. His lips teased hers, brushing the corners and nibbling gently. Then the pressure increased. Heat bubbled through her veins. The power of his kiss took over, persuaded, seduced. She trembled beneath it, feeling as if he had control of both of them. And he made her feel. Not since Kevin had any man made her feel. Just feel.

She'd never expected such softness or gentleness, or the desire curling inside her. Even as she recognized it, she didn't pull away. Caught up in the dark moist taste of him, she surrendered to a need beginning to build within her.

Stupidly she'd forgotten the madness of passion. It flowed pleasure, intense and demanding, through her. And sensations. She could have gone with them right then. That frightened her the most. With a protesting moan, she pushed at his chest, demanding space. The kiss hadn't been long. But she ached now, needs and wants alive again.

He ended the kiss with the same abruptness he'd started it. An unexpected and heavy pleasure still floating over him as he caressed her throat, pleased to feel her pulse thudding harder. "Call the police," he said before turning away. Walking away was getting harder every day. It wasn't that he was blind to the problems between them. There were a hell of a lot of them but... It was a damn big but.

Denver paced from the bed to the hotel window and squinted against the glare of a morning sun. The final rodeo competition rarely set off nerves in him. So he placed the blame where it belonged—on a woman he really had no business wanting.

From his hotel room, he could see Kelly's office building. Was she there? Was she writing about him? Hell, was she at least thinking about him? While she'd probed, he'd dug. He'd seen softness, vulnerability, compassion. When off guard, she laughed easily. When pushed too far, she struggled with a temper and showed determination. She'd revealed a patience he'd never expected, and a persistence he'd anticipated. She was exactly the kind of woman he wanted in his life, and definitely the wrong one.

Slouched in a chair, a booted foot propped on the edge of the bed, Dooley flicked to another television station. "I talked to Will last night," he said, insisting on Denver's attention.

He wondered who'd made the call, Dooley or his father. "Anxious to see Chelsea?" Denver asked.

"Go on," Dooley snarled back, and headed for the door. "There ain't nothing between us."

Except you're sweet on her, Denver mused, reaching for his shirt and following him. He had seventy-two hours at the most with a woman who'd inched her way under his skin from the beginning. At the doorway, he stopped, then whipped around. He had one phone call to make. Pride demanded he take a calculated chance and make her choose.

She couldn't let his kisses throw her off-balance, but in a strange, restless mood, Kelly spent the morning playing hooky. She did the two things she knew offered a guarantee to ease her troubled mind. She shopped, then indulged in a hot fudge sundae. Neither helped.

Strolling toward her office, she chided herself for acting almost as foolish over a man as Jamie would. Determined to forget him, she entered the huge room with its rows of desks. Letting him kiss her had been a mistake, but not a disastrous one. If she kept their relationship strictly business from now on, then—

The thought slipped away as she heard giggles behind her. Kelly looked back over her shoulder. Clearly, her co-workers were torn between idiotic smiles and unsuccessful attempts at solemnness. Why? was the big question.

Bemused, she opened the door of her office and froze in the doorway. A dozen colorful balloons danced in the air. She swayed back against the doorjamb. No matter what she did, he was determined not to get out of her life without leaving her with more memories than she'd ever wanted.

With a small shake of her head, she settled behind her desk and tried to ignore the bouncing, peach-colored balloons. No easy task. Flicking on her computer, she began work on an interview. By four-thirty that afternoon, she was still scanning the screen and fighting for the right words. The article about a movie producer didn't make sense as another man disturbed her concentration.

She sighed in disgust at herself. Hadn't Kevin taught her the danger in giving too much? Since that time with him, she'd become accustomed to being alone. She liked being her own person, making her own decisions. She hadn't looked for anything but her career. She didn't want to change her mind just because the world tilted whenever Denver kissed her.

So why couldn't she stop wondering what he was doing at that moment? Why so effortlessly did he arouse feelings that had promised to melt her?

"Ms. Shelton?" A delivery boy sauntered in. "You have to sign for this," he said, drawing her attention away from the envelope and the florist's box.

Impatient, she scribbled her name. Even before he closed the door behind him, she gave in to the excitement and had the box open. A blend of fragrances from the bright red peonies, daylilies and daisies drifted to her.

Impressed, she looked away from a lavender iris nestled amid leaves of green tissue and tore open the envelope. Two tickets for the Tchaikovsky Festival fell onto her desk. Kelly flipped open the note.

Found these and thought of you.

Denver

She dropped the tickets, feeling the heat of his touch on them. Seats had been sold out for months for this performance. That he'd pulled strings to get them for her flattered and pleased her more than the gift.

"You're frowning." Not bothering to veil her amusement at the balloons bobbing against the ceiling, Jean strolled closer and set an advance copy of this month's magazine on Kelly's desk.

"I'm stumped," Kelly admitted.

"Are you?" An eyebrow raised slightly as Jean stroked the petal of an iris. "I gather we're discussing Denver Casey."

"He's not simple."

Her aunt's eyes raised toward the balloons, then dropped to Kelly's desk, making her aware of the disarray. Almost to a fault, she was usually neat. "I never thought he would be."

Kelly tapped a finger at the magazine. "The cover looks good. The mayor's wife will be pleased with the photograph."

Her aunt nodded, perceptive eyes zeroing in on her, making Kelly feel like a ten-year-old. "Are you going to the rodeo finals?"

Kelly thought of the symphony tickets. Then she thought of Denver. He had to know if she used those tickets, she'd miss the rodeo finals. Everything would be so easy if all she felt was desire. Passion was something a person accepted or ignored. But if it was simple lust, why was she yearning just to hear the sound of his voice? Filled with confusion, she stared at her aunt. "I don't know."

Sympathetically she patted Kelly's shoulder. "Let me know. If you do, we'll go together."

He was turning her world topsy-turvy. She knew it and still she thumbed through the phone book for the hotel where he was staying.

The phone rang six times. It was just as well she hadn't reached him, she decided. He would—

She heard the click.

"Hello."

His voice floated over her. "Thank you."

For a moment, he was quiet. "Glad you liked them." He didn't indicate if he meant the balloons or the flowers or the tickets.

She gave an exasperated sigh as she stared up at the balloons. "My office looks fit for a child's birthday party."

"Festive."

The humor in his voice made her smile. "Ridiculously so. You're making me feel sixteen."

"Ah, I'm disappointed."

"With what?"

"I thought I'd be the first to send you balloons."

"You are." She leaned back in her chair. "But I'm feeling fluttery."

"Fluttery?" He drew the word out with a smile, amazed she'd confessed real feelings. "That's good news."

Kelly grabbed a quick breath. "Why are you doing this?"

"You know why."

A tremor of pleasure moved through her.

"Almost done for the day?"

She could say no. It would be easy to invent some excuse. "Yes," she said resignedly.

"I'll pick you up in—in ten minutes."

"And?"

"And we'll find something to do."

She set down the receiver, wondering if she was crazy.

He was. Half an hour later, she was standing on artificial green and playing night golf at a miniature golf course. Nearby, the music of a carousel blended with the screams of riders on a roller coaster. Visually aiming, Kelly squinted at the hole that passed through the bottom of a miniature windmill.

"Are you telling me you never came here before?" he asked, scanning the replica of a medieval castle that housed video games.

"Quit trying to distract me."

He laughed at her look of concentration. She showed the same seriousness and intensity about everything. "You're what they call a Type A. Did you know that?"

"And you're a D. Made it." She beamed back at him and swept her arm toward the windmill. "Your turn."

"There is no D." He bent forward, aimed and zipped the ball into its hole. "Only types A and B."

Kelly looked up from taking aim at the next hole. "This one is tricky."

"You have to bank it to go under the Big Ben clock."

She slanted a withering look at him. "I know that."

With a laugh, he leaned on his golf club and waited.

She winced as she missed the shot. With feigned disgust, she watched him zip the ball through the clock. "I don't understand it," she said as she aimed her final shot that had to go up a grassy knoll and land in a numbered cup.

"By my calculations, I win," he said with no graciousness at all. "What don't you understand?"

She mumbled a few choice words about beginner's luck. "You're too laid-back to be a simple B," she bantered.

He took the club from her. "You're a sore loser."

"I'm not a sore loser. You cheated. You've obviously played golf before."

Skimming her arm, he stopped at her wrist. Beneath his fingers, he felt her pulse hammering.

She let out a huge breath. "How's that?" she asked, looking up at him. "Cowboys are supposed to ride horses, not play golf."

"I'm versatile."

Kelly rolled her eyes. "Your ego is getting away from you."

He laughed, taking her comment good-naturedly. With her hand in his, he made a dash with her between fast-moving traffic.

With a grimace, Kelly looked back over her shoulder as a car whizzed by. More cautious than him, she'd have still been on the other side of the wide street waiting for a break in traffic.

"We've got a problem." Stopping her with him, he scanned the parking lot of the huge shopping mall for his truck. He couldn't remember if he'd parked in the section designated by a sign bearing a painting of oranges or the one of grapes. "This way," he said on a chance he might be right.

Kelly balked. "You parked over here," she insisted, stepping away only as far as his arm would let her.

"You're sure?"

She laughed. "I'm sure."

His knees weakened a little as the slim light of the moon slanted across her cheek and her lips almost seductively. He realized he'd have followed her even if she had been wrong.

"I never get out of a car without checking where I'm parked. When I was younger, right after I got my first car, I went shopping with my sister. It took me two hours to find the car."

"That upset you," he guessed, recalling the edge of impatience she'd shown at different times.

"Terribly." She saw no point in denying it. She'd nearly been in tears searching for it. For too many years, she'd had nothing. That car had been her first real possession.

"And your sister?"

"She laughed. She thought it was one big adventure."

He heard affection in her voice. "How is she?"

"Keeping her distance because she knows I don't approve of what she's doing. My aunt talked to her several days ago. She's withdrawn from her classes. She doesn't want to go to college anymore. Something else has snared her interest. It isn't a what. It's a who."

Denver pulled his gaze from her lips to meet her eyes. "You can't stop her from making her own mistakes."

She knew he was right. But how did a person stop worrying about someone she loved? "She's letting emotions rule her life."

He didn't know too many people who didn't. He arched an eyebrow and smiled at her. "Feelings can't be set aside so easily."

She stared at blue eyes daring her to be reckless. Before she'd met him, she'd have argued differently. "There's your car."

"I see it," he answered, but didn't take his eyes off her. "I know you want to keep clinging to that notebook of yours like it's all there is between us."

"It is—"

"Don't," he said a touch angrily. "There's been something personal between us since the first day we met. I knew it. You won't admit it."

Kelly pulled back from the hand on hers. "Denver, we really aren't meant to be together."

He sensed she wanted to run again. He had his share of reasons to dodge this, too, but he wasn't going to. If he had the guts to give it a try, why didn't she? "You keep saying that." He held a palm out to her. "So what is this then?"

She should have expected him to challenge her. He was a man used to challenging everything, used to winning. "We're together for the story, but—"

"More than for the story," he said with steely firmness.

A silence hung in the air like a thick curtain during the drive back to her apartment. She thought she knew him—an easygoing man who took life in stride. She'd been wrong. This was another side of him. Here was the intensity that had given him the drive to compete, the obstinacy that had made him a winner.

"You keep backing away," he said when he was driving into the parking lot of her apartment complex. Though she'd smiled and laughed with him, any time she felt too comfortable, she'd withdraw. Like now, he mused. "And I still don't know why."

She felt unprotected, as if he were trying to see inside her. Dodging his stare, she reached for the door handle. The iron hardness of his arm snapped across her, pinning her to the seat.

For only a second, she met his eyes, but he saw it then. Hurt. He knew now she'd been hurt. How badly? he wondered. "Kelly—"

"Let go." His touch gentled but remained firm. She saw a need to understand darkening his eyes. It had been so long since she'd talked about Kevin. Kevin, who demanded, and gave so little.

"Did someone hurt you?"

After all these years, she still felt shame, even disgust with herself for nearly repeating her mother's mistakes.

"Who hurt you?" he asked again.

She met the eyes searching hers, insisting. She could feel the steady rise and fall of his shoulder leaning against her arm. Sighing, she turned back to the window. "Someone I met in college," she said softly. "Kevin was going through medical school."

"Was it serious?"

"I thought so. He told me that we couldn't talk about marriage yet. He wanted all his plans set first. So we lived together. He thought it would be a good idea if I worked while he finished school. Then after he interned, I could go back."

Denver hunched forward to see her face.

Was it possible to explain how foolish she'd felt? She'd given one man her love unconditionally and had been made to feel used. "We didn't discuss his plans. He'd simply decided that was the way it would be. I wasn't supposed to make any decisions, only he would. I saw myself making the same mistakes my mother had, but couldn't stop myself."

The admission gnawed at her. "For two years, I worked, putting my schooling on hold and paying the bills. When he graduated, I wanted to go back to school."

She shook her head as that time in her life played out before her like a movie scene. "He said no. He said that I needed to keep working, because he'd decided to continue school and specialize."

Suddenly cold, she hugged herself. "He argued that if I loved him, I'd support his decisions. I could tell he was stunned when I didn't simply accept what he'd decided this time. I thought we'd talk more that evening. He knew how much I wanted a career, how much I needed something for myself. I thought that we loved each other, so everything would be all right."

With a finger, she traced an imaginary line down the window. "When I came home, he was gone. He'd taken everything as if I owed it all to him. Even our bank account was cleaned out. He left a note, saying he'd thought it best. He was sorry I felt the way I did, but it had been nice for a while. Nice," she said, unable to keep her anger and bitterness from surfacing.

Fragile. He'd never realized how fragile she was until that moment.

"I wondered later if he'd ever really loved me." She couldn't dodge the same intense disbelief she'd felt that dark November night. "All night I waited for him to come back. He never did." She turned eyes dulled by a sad memory on him. "For too long, I wondered how he could say he loved me, then walk away like that."

He couldn't understand it, either. Anger churned his stomach, anger directed not at her but at some selfish bastard who'd taught her the wrong lesson about sharing herself with someone. "You think I'm like him?"

That's what scared her the most, she realized. She knew that he wasn't.

"I'm not him," he said as if reading her mind.

"And I'm not that woman anymore." She hated the old feelings of rejection that had swelled up in her. "Now, I know what I do and don't want."

He leaned back, giving her space, and draped an arm over the seat behind her. "I think you do, too."

She gave him a weary smile. "You push a lot."

"I nudge," he said softly, giving into temptation and running his fingers across the slender line of her neck.

Tingling sparks shot down her with his touch that was as much of a seduction as his kisses had been.

"See me tomorrow night."

"I can't. I have to be at an art gallery," she said as a handy excuse.

"An art gallery." He frowned, his eyes roaming over her face to lips that carried a sweetness he'd never expected. More time. He needed it with her. "Okay," he said, giving her a light kiss.

"You want to go?" she asked, unable to veil her incredulity.

Of course he didn't. For her, though, he'd already willingly sat in a restaurant too stuffy to suit him. He imagined this next experience wouldn't linger as one of his favorites, either. "I want to be with you."

The huskiness in his voice quickened her pulse. Then his mouth slanted across hers again. Unhurried, his lips coaxed until hers parted. Tender. There was so much tenderness. Warmth seeped into her. Senses aroused, she clung, too aware she was yielding even more. But never before had she been kissed like this. Never had any man offered such gentleness to her. Shaken, she held on to him even when his mouth lifted from hers.

"What time should I pick you up?"

His touch and the heat of his mouth still a part of her, she felt as if she were sinking into a whirling abyss of confusion.

"What time?"

Whether she was making a mistake or not, she was doing it with her eyes open. "Seven," she said unsteadily as she hurried from the truck.

Chapter Six

Kelly spent the next afternoon at the fitness center to expel anxiety with an aerobics workout, but the only thing she accomplished was arriving home late. Rushing into her apartment, she felt an ache in her calf and winced. If exercise was so good for a person, she wondered why her body hurt so much afterward.

With a glance at the clock, she hurried through a shower and blow-drying her hair. She was nervous, really nervous, more nervous than she'd ever been before a date.

Sighing heavily she swept the hair dryer over her hair. Had she fooled herself, believing she was practical and sensible, trying to pattern herself after her aunt when she was really a romantic like her mother?

Was this how her mother had felt? Had she known Ray was wrong for her but been unable to resist?

She frowned in the mirror at herself. No, she wasn't her mother. After years of having nothing, and after too much hurt from a man who'd taken everything from her, she'd gained too much to even think of giving up all she had for any man.

Over the droning of the hair dryer, she heard the buzzer. One side of her hair still damp, she grabbed her bathrobe and scurried to open the door.

He stood at her door dressed in a dark Western-style suit, an open-collared, crisp white shirt and boots that were spit shined. He looked wonderful. Sensations that weren't comfortable ridiculously quickened her heart.

"Guess I'm early." Passing her in the doorway, he touched the wet ends of her hair.

"I'll only be a moment," she assured him and rushed toward the bedroom. Nerves pumped her blood quicker. Whether she wanted him to or not, he was pushing his way past every doubt and fear she'd had since Kevin had left her.

Visually Denver followed her quick movement down the hall, then circled the living room. Deliberately he'd come early, certain she'd give him no time to look around if he'd arrived on time. He'd seen her at work, in a high-class restaurant and at the rodeo grounds, but this was her home. He'd been only in her kitchen. He needed to see more to learn about her.

She gave the impression of sophistication. The type of woman who'd prefer smooth, sleek furniture that looked good but uncomfortable. Though she lived in a high-rent area, paying for location more than generous rooms, she'd decorated the small living room with a rocking chair and a flowered sofa. Around the room were numerous vases filled with flowers that looked as if they'd been picked from a meadow.

In passing a cherry-wood table, he stopped and picked up the photograph of Kelly and another woman, their blond heads tipped toward each other. Clearly they resembled each other, but more importantly, he saw the binding of blood in their laughing eyes. He set down the photograph and settled back against a wall to absorb everything.

As he heard the click of heels, he pivoted away from scanning the books on the shelves in the mahogany secretary. He wasn't prepared. He caught a glimpse of her hurrying through to the kitchen, a multicolored shimmery jacket in her hand. Desire closed in on him again.

Her hair pulled back and held in place by a silver comb, she was stunning in a slip of a black dress with narrow straps. He gave himself a moment to let a shaft of longing subside then drew a hard breath. Why in God's name did she have to be a reporter? Everything would have been simpler if she weren't.

Kelly ambled down the hall, slipping her lamé jacket on over the black sheath dress. "I'm ready." Head bent, she fastened the fabric button at the top of her jacket and led the way to the door. "Told you it wouldn't take long."

Reaching around her to open the door, he seemed close, so darn close she could feel the heat of his breath against her cheek as he spoke. "Nice apartment."

She needed conversation, anything to keep from concentrating on his mouth, on the dimple cutting into one corner of his cheek, on the memory of kisses she couldn't forget. "It's crowded because I keep buying and collecting. I have a closetful of patchwork quilts and needlepoints that I've done but no room for anything. But that won't be for long. I've found a house. I'm just waiting for an agreement from the sellers about the price."

"A house is important?"

He had no idea how important. A house was the final touch to have everything she'd wanted for herself since she was a young girl. "Very."

Stepping outside of the pricey apartment complex with its cobblestone walkways and replicas of Victorian lampposts, Kelly raised a hand as a breeze, warm and calm, tossed her hair. "Do you want me to drive?"

The idea of relaxing suited him. "Yeah." Opening the door for her, he placed a wispy kiss upon her eyebrow. "You're more familiar with the streets."

His hand skimmed hers before she slid into her rental car. He could make her forget, she thought, almost panicky. He could dissolve the doubts. How often without much effort had he already broken through the control she'd nurtured?

Denver had seen the frown shadowing her eyes. Settling back in the seat, he wondered what it would take to make her let go and give in to the feelings stirring between them. He knew now why she was skittish. One man, a bastard in Denver's mind, had played with her heart. But Denver wasn't that man.

He closed his eyes, not bothering to keep an eye on traffic or where they were going and enjoyed filling himself with the scent wafting to him, wondering not for the first time where she'd sprayed it.

The art gallery was crowded—couples milling around, gathering in small groups, praising paintings, sipping wine, discussing their latest cruise or trip to Europe. Until he walked in beside her.

The silence had nothing to do with his Stetson or the click of his boot heels in a room filled with women dressed in cocktail dresses and men in tuxedos. Attention riveted on him not because he was dressed differently, but because he was a celebrity, someone who'd garnered the word *champion* enough times to warrant impressing others. They wanted to hobnob with him, say they'd met and talked to him. One man, a corporate president for a local company, pumped his hand enthusiastically and rambled on about Arabian horses while his wife preened over Denver, smoothing down the lapel on his jacket just to touch him.

Denver took it all in stride. Kelly had thought he'd either be sullen and silent or fumble his way through conversation. Instead, with an ease that astounded her, he made small talk with everyone who approached him.

Working through the crowd, he touched her waist and guided her toward a painting and away from people. He felt tense, keyed up. They'd only been there minutes, and he already had his fill of the stuffy room and the buzz of conversation. Though anticipation filled him before a ride, he never felt nerves. That's what the city did to you, he reminded himself. It stressed a person. Its noise grated on a man, its buildings hid the sky and the grass and the mountains, and it zapped a man's soul with its coldness even on a sunny day.

Clearing the crowd, she heard his sigh of relief. "You should be used to that."

He gave a snort of laughter. "Never am." He kept his hand at the curve of her slim waist. At the moment, she was his foundation, the only certain thing in the room. He hated the crowds, the adoration he received for something he enjoyed.

"Stay close," she said lightly, slipping her hand in his. "I'll protect you."

He wondered if she realized that was the first time she'd reached out to touch him.

"Do you like this painting?"

He dragged his gaze away from her and toward a painting of a woman with dark hair. She and everything including trees and leaves were cast in a hue of white. He looked back at Kelly, her hair sunny, her skin golden, her nose a touch pink even under makeup. "What do you think of it?"

"You're evading again."

"I don't do that."

She laughed openly at his look of innocence. "All the time."

The smoky sound of her laugh stroked him. He wanted to pull her close, savor the taste of her. For hours, he'd thought of nothing but her and holding her.

"I like it," she said, and nearly sighed when he trailed a fingertip down the slender curve of her neck. A headiness, as if she'd drunk too much, passed over her. "It's ethereal. It's..." More intently she studied the strokes, the color, the symbolism in the Rossetti painting, but her mind was on him, close, warm, smiling at her. "It's romantic."

"Ah," he said in a teasing tone, "back to romance."

"You are single-minded," she said lightly, but she sounded breathless.

"I've been told that before." Without easing from her, he pointed to another. "I like that one."

At the touch of his hand on the small of her back, a faint wave of pleasure slithered down her spine. "It's one of Monet's most famous works."

"It makes sense. There's a sky and water and ships and people and bushes." Lightly he caressed the nape of her neck again. "You can see what he was drawing."

Curling fingers around her waist, he directed her toward the red monstrosity on the wall. "But I can't figure out for the life of me what that guy over there was on when he painted his picture. It looks like someone bled all over it."

Kelly bit back a laugh. So easily he made her smile. She realized since meeting him how much she'd laughed, how often she'd relaxed. Still smiling, she turned him with her. "Let's go over..." Her voice trailed off.

Sober looking, Greg stood near. A tall man with an angular face and a rangy build, he drew his share of admiring looks when smiling. But he scowled now. As he looked from her to Denver, she remembered her manners and made a quick introduction.

"The rodeo star." Greg arched an eyebrow. "Do sane people rodeo?"

Denver felt as if a burr were sticking him. "Except when they're on a bull." He couldn't recall jealousy ever hitting him before with such force. In eighth grade, he'd been crazy about Jana Lee Meredith, had even tumbled with Tommy Douglas over her. But this was different. No anger, just heat. Searing heat in the pit of his gut.

"Come on." Greg fastened on Kelly and curled his fingers over her arm, sloshing the wine in her glass onto her fingers. "We need to talk," he insisted, and drew her away at a pace so quick, she had to double step.

Being dragged anywhere didn't sit well with her. If they'd made a commitment of any sort to each other, she'd have understood his actions. But she knew he dated others.

"Obviously he's the one you've been seeing lately," he said angrily, the moment they were out of Denver's hearing range. "Is this a passing thing with him?"

"Excuse me?"

"I know you've been seeing him since the robbery."

"Yes, I have. You see other women," she reminded him.

He stiffened. "We're not discussing me. We're talking about you and the—the *cowboy*."

"Wait a minute." She reared back slightly. "Even if I was seeing him, you don't have a right—"

He cut in. "I don't expect to find you dating other men."

She counted slow to ten. "He agreed to an interview days ago."

His frown gave way to confusion then a semblance of a smile. "Oh, you're working. That's what this is."

It was an excuse she'd like to use, but how could she? Business and pleasure were mingling, and she didn't know where one stopped and the other began, or if they'd become one.

"Well, then," he said in a calmer tone.

While Denver was weaving a web of confusion around her, she knew one thing for certain as she met Greg's stare. The relationship she had with him didn't warrant any of this. "No, there is no more then," she said firmly.

Denver watched from a distance. He had no right to interfere, but he didn't like the tight grip Kramer had on her arm. He didn't like it one bit.

"Mr. Casey?"

He swung around, grateful for the intrusion from his own thoughts. He needed some distraction before he did something dumb. Minutes passed before he saw Kelly weaving her way through the crowd.

Her head high, she sent him a quick smile across the room. As she drew near, she used a polite excuse about introducing him to friends and whisked him away from a woman known for her loquaciousness.

"Thank you," Denver said on a quick grin. Touching the small of her back, he gave a slight jerk of his head in the woman's direction. "She sure likes to hear herself talk."

Still bristling, Kelly managed a weak smile but didn't trust herself to say too much.

His arm around her, Denver shifted so they stood inches apart. "You okay?"

She caught his glance at Greg fuming in the corner. "I'm okay." Amazingly she did feel steadier now that she was near him again. "And ready to leave."

"Where do you want to go now?" He lifted her chin with a finger to see for himself that she'd calmed. Dark eyes carried their usual sparkle. "Your choice," he said with a grin.

My choice, she mused. She cast a glance back at Greg and then looked at Denver. She sighed, feeling herself slip another notch. She realized suddenly why he was so dangerous to her. She'd found a man who understood what she needed most from him. "There's a small jazz club within walking distance of my apartment."

They sat outside at a wrought-iron table. The sound of a mellow saxophone drifted outside on the night's breeze. Kelly gave him high marks for patience. Not once since they'd left the gallery had he revealed even a vague curiosity about Greg. In her mind, the whole situation had gotten out of hand. Disturbingly, she wondered how to explain her lie at the police station about a significant other when clearly she hadn't acted as if Greg was one. Honesty works best, she reminded herself. "About what happened at the art gallery," Kelly started. "Greg usually has better manners. He thinks—well—"

"Kelly, where I'm from, a man learns where to tread so he doesn't fall in a hole."

She ran a finger down the stem of her wineglass. "You knew I wasn't telling the truth?"

"I eavesdropped when you phoned your aunt at the police station. If I'd been the man in your life, you could have called me out of the rodeo arena." Caressingly he stroked the top of her hand with his thumb. "I'd want to know you were safe." His eyes pinned hers. "What is your relationship with him?"

His question wasn't an easy one to answer. "I'm his choice for symphonies and art galleries." Kelly grimaced at the way it sounded. "Some girl named Tamara goes sailing with him. And another—I don't know her name, she does something else with him, I suppose."

Denver arched an eyebrow, stirring her laugh.

"Yes, probably that."

He gave his head a shake. "At home, men treat women right."

Bending her head, she hid a smile. "Home is Whispering Pines, isn't it?"

He watched light from the candle on the table dance shadows across her face. "You've done your homework."

"It wasn't difficult to learn where you live," she said matter-of-factly. "Why the secrecy?"

Denver resigned himself to her changed mood. "It's no big secret. Anyone can find out where I'm from.

You did." He took a hearty swallow of his beer. "If I don't broadcast it, it's to protect others." There was more truth in those words than she'd guessed. "It's my home. Would you want strangers tramping around outside your home?"

His propensity for privacy sounded amazingly logical to her. "No, I wouldn't," she admitted. "Will you go home after the rodeo?"

"I'm expected." He grinned wryly. "If I have even three days between rodeos, I go home. I never got the hang of city living."

Finally, sentences with *I* in them. Kelly needed little encouragement. "Did you want to?"

At the eagerness in her voice, he couldn't help but smile. "I've been to enough cities over the past ten years, trying to figure out what's so great about them."

"For a man who likes country living, why would you?"

"My mother was from the city." He looked up to see her gaze steady on him. What the hell. She'd shared. Maybe it was time for him to give something back. "My father met her when she was sixteen. She'd been crowned queen of something for the county," he said, knowing if she wanted to learn details, they were available to the public. "By the time she'd turned twenty-one, she'd won several beauty contests and had started modeling. He came to Phoenix for the livestock show and began pursuing her until she agreed to marry him."

"Sounds romantic."

The blue eyes he raised to her were solemn. "Only sounds that way." He continued before she cornered him with a question he didn't want to answer. "Country life isn't easy. Isolation, the sameness can bore someone looking for excitement. She'd had a taste of city life. I was twelve when they got divorced."

Though he'd worked up a casual tone, Kelly didn't buy it. At twelve, his world must have shattered. Divorce was harder on children than people realized. They lost the certainty and the stability in their lives. They questioned themselves, worrying they were to blame. And they were forced to choose. No matter what the circumstances of the divorce, the child had to choose.

She wanted to be detached, but during a few quiet moments, he'd drawn her in, telling her something that she sensed was still difficult for him. "Where did she go?"

He'd never give everything, not to her, not to anyone. "To the city to live with a cousin. I was used to the ranch, country living. Her world, the one she longed for, seemed foreign to me. I wanted no part of it then. But later, I got curious to see what my mother thought was so exciting, so I gave the city a try."

Nearby, a car horn blared. He longed for the howl of a coyote. Surrounding them rose concrete and glass skyscrapers. A yearning filled him for the sight of the mountains near his ranch. "It's still not my speed."

During the return trip to her apartment, Kelly considered what he'd told her. Though they'd led such different lives in a way, they were kindred souls, linked by the insecurity and the shadows of childhood heartache. "You're anxious to go home, aren't you?" she asked when they reached the outer door of her apartment building.

A smile hovered at the corners of his lips. "Not as anxious as I used to be."

His eyes, shadowed by the mantle of night, looked darker, more intense. "Denver..." She paused a moment as his hand cupped the back of her neck. "I never wanted to get involved with you."

He knew she'd made that decision long ago. She wasn't a spontaneous woman. In a way, that trait enticed him more. He'd been born and raised in a setting where without careful planning, a person could starve, a business could fold during one stormy winter. "Who did you say that for?" he asked in that slow easy drawl that charged something inside her. "To convince me or yourself?"

He read her too well. She stared at his mouth and wasn't able to think about anything but the pleasure she knew she'd find in his kiss. "Both of us."

As she pulled away and whirled around to retrieve her mail from the slot, Denver started to grab her. Within the time it took to draw a breath, whatever else he planned to say was cast aside. He watched her pale and inched closer. "What's wrong?"

For a long moment, Kelly stared at one of the envelopes. A plain white envelope with no address or postmark.

"Maybe..." He gave up the idea of suggesting she handle the envelope carefully. She'd already ripped it open. He peered over her shoulder to read the note.

Forget what you saw. I'll be watching you.

She released a shuddery breath. She was scared, more frightened than she'd ever been. "I thought it would stop."

He slouched to see her face better. She was breathing hard, alarm visible in her eyes. "Did you tell the police about the phone calls?"

With effort, Kelly straightened her backbone. "No. Nothing was said. There was no way to know who made those calls."

Perhaps it was because she was defiant, struggling for strength, or because he needed her close to assure himself she was safe that he drew her into his arms. Never did he doubt that they'd be lovers. What he hadn't expected was the need to protect her filling him. "Call the police."

"I will."

"Now," he insisted, aware his own heart was still beating a touch faster.

Stubbornly, she warred with panic. "After you leave, I'll call."

He framed her face with his hands and kissed her hard. There was no coaxing this time. Insisting and demanding, his lips twisted across hers. She struggled to keep emotions from going wild. She wasn't an impulsive woman. She wasn't the kind to have a brief affair with any man. She didn't want some man in her life who shifted the ground when he kissed her. But she closed her eyes, responding to a kiss that wasn't gentle or soft this time.

As he took his fill of her, she gave in. She'd been yearning, wanting this again. All the denials seemed useless. She was beginning to need, truly need this man. No man had ever made her feel quite this way. Not even Kevin, she realized. Repeatedly, Denver detonated something inside her she couldn't ignore. She tasted heat. A consuming heat. It seemed to engulf her, burning her skin, searing her lips.

Madness. It was all madness, she told herself. But when had she ever stood with any man, nearly aching for the feel of his arms around her and the touch of his lips? She heard her own sigh and knew she was close, very close to yielding.

That she trembled pleased him. Strangely he understood her wariness. But the mouth answering his wasn't apprehensive. It carried a different message. He could force the moment; he wouldn't. Though she might feel desire, she wasn't desperate with it yet. He wanted it all with her. Drawing back, he felt her breathing hard. He was just as breathless, but he took her mouth once more. Tenderly. More than desire made him linger. This wasn't a passion he understood. He tried to memorize the sweet womanly taste of her, the heat of her body. He fought his own tug-of-war. "It's too late to tell me you didn't want that," he said huskily. "That you don't want more."

His words danced like a caress across her skin. His taste still lingering on her lips, her blood still warm from his kiss, she opened the door.

Cursing at some man he'd never met, a man who'd left her with scars, he watched her rush from him.

Chapter Seven

Kelly wasn't certain what unnerved her more, her feelings for Denver or her fear since last night's threatening note. The police hadn't eased her mind. One of them had met her at her office. After a glance at the note, the detective had requested she come with him to look at a lineup. In passing, he told her what she'd already guessed. The brothers were using scare tactics.

Amazingly, she hid her anxiety from her aunt despite the older woman's insistence on answers. "Were you able to identify the gunman?" At Kelly's nod, her aunt paced her office. "So they've arrested him?" She stopped, sighing heavily. "I should be relieved to hear that, but I'm more worried now."

"Don't be. I'm not." Liar, her mind screamed while she feigned a bright smile for her aunt.

Only later, when leaving her aunt's office, did she admit how frightened she was. She'd done exactly what the note had warned her not to do.

She knew better than to let her mind play games with her or paranoia might set in. But if she avoided pondering the threat, she automatically thought about Denver. She stared at the tickets for the symphony. Not once yesterday had he asked if she was coming to the rodeo. Again, he was giving her space. No, he was making her choose.

She picked up the notes she'd jotted down about him. The story wasn't complete. She felt that instinctively, but with him going back to Whispering Pines soon, she'd never get a complete picture of him now.

Riffling through pages of notes, she mumbled a soft curse. She'd always prided herself on being thorough, but somehow, she'd forgotten to have him sign a photo release.

In a way, that was explainable. Who could think straight with dozens of balloons dancing around her? Leaning forward, she propped her elbows on her desk as a feeling of frustration drifted over her.

It was because of those balloons, she insisted. Silly, peach-colored... She leaned back, frowning. Why were they all peach-colored? What was so significant about the color peach that he'd sent her two dozen balloons that color?

It wasn't that she didn't like them. They reminded her of a suit she'd bought... Peach. It was peach. She'd taken it to the cleaners the day after the robbery. Had he been remembering her in that suit? Had he been thinking about her since that day?

Oh, God, she desperately wanted to be sensible, and she suddenly knew she wouldn't be. Picking up the telephone receiver, she punched out numbers quickly, not giving herself time to change her mind.

She listened to several rings before Greg answered. He sounded predictably annoyed at being disturbed at the bank. Kelly didn't allow him to voice his displeasure. "I have two tickets for tonight's performance at symphony hall. Would you like them?"

"Is this an apology?"

She clenched her teeth for a moment. "A friendly gesture. Would you like the tickets?"

"For the Tchaikovsky Festival? How did you get them?"

"A friend. I'll leave them in my mailbox for you."

"You're not going?"

"No, I have other plans."

He sounded bewildered. "What could possibly be more enjoyable?"

She laughed at herself. "A rodeo."

With plans for her aunt to pick her up at five-thirty, Kelly rode the elevator down from her apartment. She stepped outside and stared in disbelief.

Beaming, her aunt greeted her from inside a limousine. "We're traveling in style."

Aware she was gaping, Kelly shut her mouth quickly and stepped forward. "What are you doing in that?"

"Denver sent a car for me. Odd, he didn't think you were going. But wasn't that nice of him?"

Kelly felt walls closing in on her. "Whoever heard of a cowboy hiring a limousine?" she said, settling in beside her aunt.

Jean laughed, seeming to enjoy the moment, and fingered the fringe on Kelly's suede blouse. "You look as if you were meant to wear those clothes."

Uncharacteristically, Kelly slouched back on the seat. She was losing a battle that she didn't even want to fight anymore.

Country music greeted them. Blaring from a public address system, it mingled with the whinny of horses, the buzz of the crowd gathering.

"Shall we get into the spirit of this and buy a bag of popcorn or peanuts or..."

Kelly laughed at her aunt's efforts to do what was expected. No doubt she felt more out of place than Kelly had the first time she'd strode onto the fairgrounds toward the rodeo arena. "I'm for peanuts."

While her aunt went to the concession stand, Kelly ambled past the stock pens. It was easy to admire the animals, muscled and well trained; their riders, determined and heady with the excitement of competition.

"Did you come with your aunt?"

She turned the moment he spoke. "A limo picked us up." She gave him a wry smile, her eyebrows knitting. "You're unpredictable."

He'd been struggling to think about competition, and all the while waiting to see if she'd come. "What did you do with the symphony tickets?"

She knew he'd ask. "I found someone who wanted to go there more than I did." She was trying to come to terms with her own actions. She'd learned not to need a man, not to put too much time or effort into a relationship, not to expect too much. Yet, given a choice, she'd chosen to be near him.

"Denver?"

He looked back to see Dooley smirking. Nearby, men stretched their stirrups, taped wrists and checked ropes. Everyone was thinking about competition except him. "I have to go." The casual tone was an act. He wanted to kiss her until everything he was feeling seeped into her. "I'll see you after."

"Good luck."

He stalled in turning away. What the hell. Burying his hands in her hair, he took her mouth in his.

Unprepared, she melted against him as he deepened the kiss. It lasted only a moment, but it was long enough to rush that damn fluttery sensation through her again.

"Thanks," he said and walked away.

She stood still for a long moment, feeling more vulnerable than she had in years. At the hum of whispers surrounding her, she drew a hard breath and swung around.

Jean strolled toward her, her eyes dancing with a smile. "You have a glow about you that I don't recall ever seeing before," she said, obviously in no mood for subtlety.

Kelly vowed not to blush like a teenager. "I'm sunburned."

"Oh, is that what it is?" Her aunt's smile widened. "Yes, your nose is sunburned."

Together they inched their way to their seats. Kelly was glad to sit down. Whether he'd been pursuing with the tenacity of a bulldog or offering a sympathetic word about her sister or a gentle touch when she'd been anxious, he'd always made her react.

Settling back, she took in the sights and sounds, the atmosphere, the people at the rodeo. She had no answers about what she felt for him. She'd like to write it off as sexual attraction, but he possessed more than good looks. He was a gentle man, a compassionate and caring one. To be honest, he was downright wonderful. She couldn't imagine too many women resisting him.

"It's starting," Jean said, insisting on her attention.

Around them, the smell of beer and hot dogs permeated the air. Kelly studied the arena as the barrel-racing competition began.

One after another, the horse and rider charged forward after the drop of a flag to round barrels, then galloped back to the finish line in a race against time.

Though the action interested her, she kept searching for Denver. Stopped, talking to another participant, he tipped his hat back and rubbed the knuckle of his thumb between his eyebrows. Something was annoying him, she concluded. Several times, she'd seen him... She let the thought flutter away with the realization that she'd noticed a habit of his.

With his glance up at her, she guessed what was bothering him. *She* was. The feeling was mutual.

"Do you want to talk?" Jean asked, assuring Kelly the exchange hadn't gone unnoticed.

Kelly wondered if it would do any good to pretend there wasn't a problem.

"It could be he's not an ordinary cowboy."

Kelly heard the humor in her aunt's voice. He wasn't ordinary at anything. That was the problem. He belonged in a world she wanted no part of, but disturbingly, she knew she wanted to be with him.

As the crowd jolted to a stand when a bronc jumped out of a chute, she rose automatically, too. Excitement rippled across the stands, spectators hanging on the action of the bronc shooting upward, rocking his rider. A collective groan resounded with the rider sprawling to the ground.

Another rider's luck wasn't better than the previous one's. His bronc stormed straight for the fence. At it, the horse twisted around. The rag-doll cowboy flew in the air, then thumped to the ground.

Engrossed in the performances, Jean took a hearty bite of a hot dog. "Some junk food is good," she mumbled, drawing Kelly's laugh.

With the announcement of the bull riding, the crowd stirred. Denver had already drawn good marks in two of the events. Adrenaline pumping through her for his final event, she concentrated on the riders and their marks.

The first rider was flung forward on the bull. He didn't last a few seconds before being tossed off. He scrambled out of the way of the bull's hooves and dashed for the fence. Dejected, his shoulders slumping, he beat the dust from his hat against the fence.

Contestant after contestant pitted himself against the bone-racking rides. Some succeeded, some failed, venting their frustration by stomping on their hats or slamming a fist into the ground after being thrown. But applause greeted all of them, the crowd respecting their effort.

"Denver's up next," her aunt informed her unnecessarily.

She'd already noticed him near the chute area. Wedged in one of them was a Brahman bull hell-bent on escaping his pen. Denver poised, perching precariously over it, then eased onto the bull's back. He raised one arm and nodded to the gatekeeper.

The instant the gate swung open, the bull exploded, charging forward in a puff of dust. The animal rose into the air, then thumped his feet to the ground. Kelly heard the yells of the crowd as Denver's body whipped around. Unmercifully, the bull jumped and spun to deliver a bone-jarring ride, but he hung tight, outriding the buzzer.

Among the following six riders, four fared well; two didn't.

On her feet with the others, Kelly watched Denver dart into the arena and wave his hat in answer to the announcement of his name and the resounding applause. Her heart beating harder, she stilled at clapping her hands as something akin to pride swept through her. She hummed with it. She wanted to pretend she'd been caught up in the crowd's jubilant reaction, but her heart hammered out a different message. Her feelings were different than those of the masses acknowledging his performance.

Stunned, she dropped back to her seat, aware that he'd aroused still another emotion in her. One that was meant for someone near and dear to her heart.

He'd won, she mused. More than the contest. But no matter what happened between them, somehow, she'd protect herself from being hurt again.

Hat in hand, Denver strode from the arena and around the livestock pens. Pats on the back followed him as he inched his way past a crowd of well-wishers.

A willowy blonde leaned into him and pecked his cheek. "I'd love to celebrate with you."

Impatience rose within him to get clear of the crowd and her. He managed a smile, slipped free of her grip and politely nudged past people. All the while, he searched the sea of faces for one woman's.

Falling in step with him, Dooley offered him a can of soda. "You been seeing a lot of her."

Denver took a long swallow to clear away the taste of dust in his mouth.

"Can you trust her?"

It was a question he'd been asking himself for days.

A crowd meandered toward their cars. Clouds thick with moisture hung overhead, stirring the breeze, threatening rain.

Walking at a leisurely pace, Kelly listened to her aunt's replay of the rodeo. "I truly, truly enjoyed myself," she gushed.

Kelly was as surprised as her aunt sounded. "I'm glad to hear that."

With a distracted look at her wristwatch, Jean frowned. "I promised to meet someone ten minutes ago."

"Someone?"

Jean gave her a sly smile. "Someone."

Kelly played good sport. "Then take the limo."

"How will you get home?"

"I'm sure I can get a ride."

"Well, then." Her eyes a touch brighter, she hugged Kelly's shoulder and said a breezy goodbye.

Odd, but Kelly couldn't ever recall her aunt having a date. Pushing her sunglasses to the top of her head, she watched the limo pulling away, then swung around and started toward Denver's truck. She was halfway there when he fell in step beside her.

"You're all alone?"

"My aunt had to leave early, so I need a ride." She wanted to hug him. Instead, uncertain, she leaned closer to kiss his cheek lightly. "Congratulations." A casual gesture, she told herself. A token of congratulations. Except she wasn't feeling casual toward him.

Touched, he ran a hand down her arm. The win placed second in his mind. Even before competition had begun, he'd known that the real prize he'd been after was seeing her here. "I had good draws." He caught her hand. "Did your aunt enjoy it?"

As the warmth of his hand penetrated hers, an acceptance slithered over her. "Loved it."

Without missing a stride, he plopped his hat on her head. "It looks good on you."

She sent him a skeptical look. "I only have your word for that."

"Trust me." The words echoed in his mind during the drive to her apartment. Aside from his ranch family, he couldn't count on one hand the people he trusted. And not one of them was a woman.

Kelly shifted toward him on the seat. "You're awfully quiet. You won," she reminded him lightly.

"It's the coming-down syndrome," he said as an excuse. Could he trust her? No woman had ever made him wonder that before.

Kelly looked out the window at the drizzling rain. "Do you feel a high before competition?"

"Always. It's something I work on."

"I do the same thing, too," she said, somewhat amazed that two so different occupations required the same preparation. "Before I talk to someone, I do a lot of research on them. If the person is a writer, I read one of the author's books. If it's a movie star, I see one of their movies. I try to work up enthusiasm. What do you do?"

"I cuss out the bull."

She slanted a smile at him. "Do you really?"

"Yeah, I do." He parked in the lot of her apartment complex and turned off the ignition. "I go to the livestock pens and have a talk with him."

Amusement crept into her voice. "You tell him who's boss?"

Rain quickened, drumming against the roof of the truck. "Sometimes," he said, opening his door.

His arm around her, he huddled her close as they dashed through the parking lot and into the building. "And sometimes, he doesn't listen."

Stepping into the elevator with him, she laughed and stared up at his face dripping with water. Without thinking, she brushed her fingertips across his cheek. "Can I admit something to you and not hear I-told-you-so?"

He smelled the rain on her. "Promise."

"I enjoyed the rodeo more than I expected to."

"Quite an admission."

"Yes, I thought so," she said, feigning a serious look and drawing his smile.

As they stepped out of the elevator, Denver took her keys from her. "Did you tell the police about the note?"

Kelly nodded like an obedient child. "Yes, I did." She arched an eyebrow. "They weren't surprised."

Grimacing, he unlocked the door and pushed it open for her. "That's not comforting."

In passing, she flicked on the stereo because the apartment seemed too quiet. "No, I didn't think so, either. But they didn't think they could prove the brothers..." She stopped talking, feeling as if she was drowning beneath his stare. Suddenly nothing felt steady. "Have you noticed that they keep asking the same questions all the time?"

Busy talk, Denver mused. And all the while, desire crackled between them with a look or a touch. He felt it.

So did she. She flitted around the room, turning on a lamp, setting her briefcase on the table, digging in it for who knows what.

"I have a release form for the photographs that you have to sign."

He watched her mouth, thought of her taste. "It can wait."

Kelly looked up. "Aren't you supposed to be somewhere for a celebration?"

He crossed to her at the table and took her hand. "I'm where I want to be."

The softness in his voice swept a tingle through her.

"I knew you weren't like other women I'd met," he said softly. Her eyes looked dark to him, vulnerable, and still a touch uncertain. "I want you. I won't deny that. But..." How would he explain? They hadn't known each other long, yet it was as if there had never been another woman in his life. She'd done more than inch her way under his skin. She was a part of his thoughts constantly. She was close to his heart. "You've never been easy to understand."

His fingers brushed her cheek with a touch that was so tender she nearly swayed into it. Heat warmed her blood as memories of his kisses, of the quickening of her heart, swarmed in on her. Had she ever wanted like this before? she wondered.

He slid his hand over hers. For a moment, he stared at the delicate fingers. He ached to feel her touching him. "I don't know the answer to this, but I could stay in Phoenix for a while."

Her heart thudded so hard she thought it might stop at any moment. He was offering to stay where he really didn't want to be to give them more time. "And then?"

"I don't know." Linking his fingers with hers, he drew her around the table with him. "Do you want an answer to that?"

She was afraid of one. In the distance she heard the crack of lightning, yet all she could think about was a different storm simmering within her. "What are we doing?"

Like a butterfly's caress, his mouth grazed her cheek as he pressed a hand lightly at the curve of her waist. "Dancing. I've never danced with you."

Desire darkening his eyes, he held her with a look. She knew a moment of truth was closing in on her. With a simple brush of his lips across her forehead, he'd soothed her frustration over her sister. Not with passion but with the tenderness and the compassion of a friend, he'd held her close after the threats. Because of him, she'd been able to lean on someone for the first time in years.

As he gently touched her face, a sense of how right this was washed over her. She needed to be with him. She didn't know what would happen between them. All she wanted was to go with the emotion he touched inside her.

"Tell me what you want," he urged.

The decision was hers, she reminded herself. With the caress of his mouth at the corner of her lips, and his breath, warm and sweet, fanning her face, a wild rush of pleasure swept through her. This time she'd have her eyes wide open though. She'd look for no promises, expect nothing but the joy of the moment. But she did want that much with him.

"Tell me," he insisted.

She placed a hand against his chest and felt his heart beating at the same quick pace as her own. "You," she whispered against his lips. "I want you." Her arms coiling around his neck, she sighed against his mouth, straining into him. She knew she wasn't sensible or foolish. She was simply a woman aching for one particular man. Nothing mattered but the taste of him. A sound slipped out filled with pleasure as his hand skimmed over her. The rain drummed against the window, but all she heard was the wild pounding of her heart.

She tasted the rain on him, touched the moisture in his hair as her tongue met his and explored. She'd tried to stay detached by avoiding such moments with any man. But he wasn't just any man. With him, she felt reckless. For him, she'd take this chance. However long this was meant to last, she'd accept the moments, anticipate no more.

He checked an urge to rush. For too long, he'd imagined a moment like this. With care, he opened the buttons on her blouse. His eyes never leaving hers, he slipped it from her. Silk whispered beneath his fingers. Still, he moved slowly.

Framing his face with her hands, she obeyed each subtle touch of his hand, shifting slightly to help him free her of her clothes. Desire curled around him. He fought it, too aware of how delicate she really was. He wanted to go slow, to savor. But he felt as if he'd been waiting for this moment forever.

Need building within him, he kissed her again and swept her into his arms. When they floated to the bed, his mouth was on hers. She fueled him, her hands helping him shrug out of his shirt, roaming along his back to his waist, tugging at the buckle of his belt, at damp denim, shoving it from his hips, her feet kicking it free. Soft. Pliant. She was offering a willingness he'd never expected. There was an insistence in the lips clinging to his, prompting him to take what he wanted.

Kisses lengthened, each blending into the next. She didn't think. She could only feel. Closing her eyes, she lost herself in him, her skin tingling beneath the caress of his hands and mouth. As he kissed her breast, then caught a nipple, stroking it with his tongue, heat stormed her.

With each hot kiss that trailed down from her breasts to her stomach, then lower, she opened more to him. With a soft moan, she writhed beneath him, not to escape but to arch upward. She caught her breath, and as he fed on her, she clutched at him. Nothing had ever been like this, she thought in a lucid moment. In the time it took to draw a breath, she was drowning in pleasure. She wouldn't think about tomorrow. Breathless, her skin growing damp with passion, she murmured his name. Tonight, only tonight mattered.

For the first time in his life, he wondered if he'd ever satisfy the craving for a woman's taste. He watched a shuddering wave pass over her before he slipped his hands beneath her hips. With the full length of her, naked and warm, pressed against him, there was no hope for slowness now.

Nothing seemed like enough. She filled his mind. A burning led him to please her, to make her as much a servant to the clawing ache as he was. It came quickly. The demand, the hunger, the urgency.

As she gasped, he moved in her, against her. He heard her whimper his name, felt her mouth against his shoulder. The touch of her hands stroking his back coaxed him. The sound of her pleasure echoing in his head drove him. His ragged breathing blending with hers, he yielded to the madness taking hold. In a second of time, he knew that now wouldn't be enough. It was his last thought before they melted together.

Chapter Eight

It wasn't the soft patter of rain but her scent that stirred him. Even before he opened his eyes, he was aware of dawn's light and the warm body beside him under the jumble of sheets. He buried his face in her hair and floated a hand down her bare hip. He'd been awake for minutes, finally thinking again. About her. About goodbyes. About how easily she could hurt him. Never would she know that he was just as vulnerable as she. Too many ghosts of the past had shadowed him, too. Until he'd met her, they'd haunted him. Until her, he'd given only part of himself to any women. For her, he might give everything. "Are you awake?"

"Barely," she murmured, wiggling closer and accepting the tightness of his arms around her. She felt languid, her body wonderfully tired. Passion. It would be enough. It had to be, she convinced herself, stroking the faint line of hair down his belly.

Lazily he shifted to see her face and propped himself on an elbow. Silk. She'd been soft as silk everywhere. "You're beautiful."

She'd heard similar compliments before. Why did it seem so different from him? she wondered as she traced a fingertip up his ribs. She'd never given so much. She'd never received so much, she realized, remembering how she'd reached for him in the middle of the night and how quickly the pleasure had rushed over her. She knew that their worlds were different. So how was it possible that two people so wrong for each other could blend so perfectly? "And you're..." Stilled by his wince, she raised her eyes to his.

"Battle wounds. Ignore them," he murmured against her throat.

Curiously she outlined a jagged scar at the edge of his hipbone. "And this?"

"A souvenir from a bull." His knee throbbed, still sore from yesterday's competition, and though the brush of her body rubbed a bruise at his hip, he welcomed the warmth of her, a comfort for the other aches in his body. Already because of her leisurely touch, heat was beginning to flow through him again. The wanting had been satisfied, but what about his need for her? It was stronger, even more intense now. He remembered the giving, the sound of her soft moans. Excitement, weakness, power, he'd felt it all with her. "Weren't you about to say something like I'm wonderful?"

Smiling, she traced the dimple in his cheek. "I could say that."

Softly he laughed, his breath fanning her lips. "Go ahead. I can take it."

"You've heard those compliments before."

"None of them ever meant anything until this moment." Against him, he felt her catch her breath. "No line." Lightly he kissed the bridge of her nose, the frown marring her forehead. "It was special last night."

She curled into him and closed her eyes. Her hand on his chest, she felt the steadiness of his breaths. For a moment longer, emotions dominated her. She was tempted to snuggle. There was more danger in that than all of the kisses and caresses they'd shared through the night. Need that had nothing to do with desire left a woman weak, too vulnerable. Drawing back, she smiled at him, then eased away, snatching up the nearest available clothing.

The instant she'd left his side, Denver lazily willed himself from going back to sleep. Folding an arm beneath his head, he enjoyed the view of her crossing the room, wearing only his shirt. He'd have liked her to stay beside him. He sensed she was already trying to separate herself not only from him but also the feelings binding them after a night together.

Kelly sneaked a glance at him. She felt the self-consciousness of morning. Though the rain still pattered against concrete, daylight seemed too bright, too filled with the chance of promises that had nowhere to go. It had been so much easier last night. Night swallowed everything real. Now, she was faced with the uncertainty of everything that had happened. "I think you should get up," she said, trying to sound steady when she wasn't sure of anything.

"Later."

At his seductive drawl, she looked over her shoulder. In her bed, his dark head against the feminine eyelet pillowcase, he looked too content to move. "Aren't you going to get up?"

A pleasurable expression settled on his face. "Later."

She tilted her head. "Is that all you can say?"

With a finger, he beckoned her. "Come here." Desire was so much a part of him, he didn't think he could move.

His lazy smile more than his request tempted her. Her bottom lip caught between her teeth, she stifled a smile and knelt on the bed beside him. In amusement, she looked down as he slowly unbuttoned the shirt. "No, I think you should get up," she said, aware of how easily his hands could make her quiver again.

"I might get up if..." He gave her a quick kiss.

Smiling, Kelly braced a hand against his chest to keep from being pulled down. "If what?"

"If you'd meet me in the shower."

"In the—"

With a gentle nudge, he shoved her back onto the mattress, then scrambled over her and out of the bed.

Kelly caught only a glimpse of his bare backside. Laughing, she took off and trailed him down the hallway. A step behind, she shoved him out of the way with her hip. "You don't race fair," she said between breaths.

He gave her room, swaying to the right to let her pass.

She should have sensed his sneaky nature, but proud of herself, she beamed with satisfaction over her shoulder at him. "I win."

Only a second passed. One step from the bathroom doorway, she let out a squeal as her feet were lifted from the floor.

Holding her tight in his arms, he gave her a cocky grin. "I win."

She wondered if they both had. "You win," she agreed, coiling her arms around his neck.

Rain drummed harder. Setting down the hair dryer, she stared at her reflection in the bathroom mirror. She looked different. Glowy. Was there such a word? No, she didn't think so, but something about her was different.

She followed the sound of whistling to the kitchen. In the faint light of it, he stood in only his jeans, his hair still damp from the shower. Almost lovingly she visually traced the scar on his back. He'd made the morning after so easy. She'd been tense, uncertain. As usual, he hadn't been. Smiling at his earthy curse about the empty cupboards, she leaned against the doorjamb. "Coffee is all I have."

With a quick sidestep, he closed the refrigerator door, then crossed to her, backing her up against the counter. "We're in trouble." Lightly he grazed the curve of her hip. "The way I see it," he murmured against the corner of her mouth, "we have two choices, or we're going to starve."

Feeling young and a touch silly, she slid her arms around his neck and pressed closer. "I can hardly wait to hear them."

He smiled at the rare teasing in her voice. "You could dress, and I'll take you out for breakfast."

She shivered beneath the sensuous trace of his fingertips along her thigh. She breathed deeply, the clean male scent of him filling her mind. Her lover. He was her lover. She was still trying to adjust to that.

"Or stay like you are." He tugged at the tie on her robe, stirring her giggle. "And I'll bring something back, and then—"

"And then, sounds wonderful," she said on a laugh, stroking his jaw and the stubble of his beard. "But I'll get dressed and go with you." She slipped under his arm. "I know a great deli," she called back.

He reached the bedroom door to see her yanking a T-shirt over her head. "It's raining. Why should both of us get wet?"

"I don't mind," she mumbled while trying to find her way through the shirt. She popped her head through the neck of it. Say it, her mind urged. Say what you feel. "I'd rather be with you."

He didn't take her words lightly. Despite intimacy with him, he knew she was a woman afraid to let go. "How far is the deli?"

"We can walk there."

Denver reached for his shirt. "It's still raining."

"So?" In passing, she stroked the back of his hair. "We won't melt," she said, laughing as she sidestepped his lunge for her. "I like walking in the rain."

* * *

"How far is this place?" Denver asked when they stepped outside minutes later and rain hurled at them.

Tipping back her head, she let the raindrops plop onto her face. "Not far. Half a block."

It was a moment like this one, her smiling with childlike joy at something as simple as rain, that he'd been waiting for.

The rain pounded harder, forcing them to dash for the deli. As they stepped in, a bell above the door jingled. It was a narrow room with Formica tables and chairs parallel to the long display counter. Behind it, a short woman with salt-and-pepper hair waved a salami at them. "Rain, rain, rain," she grumbled with a Yiddish accent. "It's not good for business." She rounded the counter and touched Kelly's cheek affectionately. "We can count on our favorite people, though."

Denver wiped the rain from his face and noted the lone potted plant in a far corner. "You're a regular here?"

"I have to eat somewhere." Kelly stripped off her raincoat and hung it on a coatrack near the door. "And like I said—"

"You rarely eat at home."

"Yes." She inched along the display counter, eyeing the chocolate torte.

"You're going to have some of the cheesecake today?" the woman said.

Kelly eyed it, then glanced at the chocolate torte.

With a look of disbelief that she was even considering it, Denver ran fingers through his wet hair. "She's kidding, isn't she?"

Kelly swiveled her head to look back at the cheesecake. "No. I usually have it or the carrot cake or—"

He pressed a fingertip to her lips to silence her. "How about something more normal this morning."

"More normal?"

Denver perused the cardboard menu behind the counter. "Waffles," he suggested. "How about waffles?"

"Great idea. Belgian waffles. A favorite of mine. Piles of whipped cream," she instructed the woman behind the counter.

With a shake of his head, he sat back on a table and grinned. "Hold the whipped cream on mine," he called out.

"Delicious, aren't they?" she mumbled, taking another hearty bite. She looked around her, realizing it was one of the few times in months she'd sat in her kitchen with anything other than a cup of coffee.

Cautiously Denver sipped the steaming brew in his cup. "Almost as good as Lorna's."

Across the table from him, she cocked an eyebrow. "Who's Lorna?"

"Prettiest woman in Whispering Pines."

At the tease dancing in his eyes, she wagged her fork at him. "Oh, really?"

"A beautiful silver-haired lady with a tongue that's sharp enough to keep any cowpoke in line." He grinned. "She's Charlie Barnes's wife. He's the cow boss at the ranch. Like your aunt, she's a special lady."

She matched his smile and dipped her fork into the mound of whipped cream. "Do you miss the ranch?"

"Always have," he said between bites.

"Does Charlie handle it when you're gone?"

Denver held down a grin. How could anyone think of so many questions? "My dad does."

Kelly slid another piece of the waffle into her mouth. "You're close?"

"We're close," he said with a nod.

"And your mother?"

Inwardly, Denver tensed. Because of the closeness with her during the past twenty-four hours, he'd almost forgotten the magazine story she sought. "When she left, I figured she was out of my life."

Until that moment, she'd been passing casual conversation. The flat emotionless tone of his voice made her look up from her plate. "Why?"

Denver set down his fork and met eyes filled more with compassion than curiosity. "She wanted no part of my world, so I wanted nothing from her."

He'd been hurt, and deep down, he was still hurting. "A difficult choice."

He shook his head and pushed back his chair. "I never regretted it." Rubbing at one side of his shoulder to ease the burning pain, he walked into the living room and dropped to the sofa with the newspaper. He'd given her a piece of himself that no one else had ever had. Over the top of the newspaper, he eyed the small vases filled with an array of wildflowers, the salt-and-pepper shaker collection displayed behind the glass of a small curio cabinet. Silently he cursed. Warm, welcoming, her apartment reminded him too much of home.

Kelly slanted a look at him. By his frown, she was sure he was wondering about his having confided so much in her. She could have reassured him. None of that was anyone else's business, but had his life on the rodeo circuit stemmed from a yearning to understand his mother? Did he have feelings for his mother beyond the visible coldness? It was a side of him no one ever saw, a side that didn't fit the man who gave reverence to a rodeo clown, who offered advice to competitors, who crooned to a friend's baby. She wondered if such indifference was real or his way of anesthetizing himself from the pain.

A cup in hand, she joined him on the sofa, wishing she could take back the past few moments that had snatched away his smile. She sensed he hadn't told her everything, but she wasn't sure she really wanted to know it all. For a moment, he'd opened himself to her. She knew passion alone didn't bridge the way to such intimacy. Something else was happening. With her fingertip, she traced one of the deep grooves bracketing his mouth. "Did you know I was a sucker for dimples?"

At the smile in her voice, he looked up. He wanted nothing spoiling the moment, especially his own dark mood. "Could have fooled me."

She laughed as the grooves deepened. "Well, I couldn't make things too easy for you."

"Easy?" He laughed. "That you didn't."

Satisfied, she snuggled closer as he draped an arm around her shoulder. "Do you always read a newspaper from back to front?"

"That's what some lefties do."

"Backward, are you?" She tangled a foot with his and settled back again against him to read the newspaper he held. For the fourth time, she perused a column about the latest acquisition to the Phoenix Suns. "Are you ever going to turn the page? We've been reading this same one for five minutes."

Amused, he kissed the top of her head, then stroked her shoulder, almost feeling obsessed for any kind of contact. "Let's try teamwork, so I don't have to use my other hand."

She tilted a look up at him. "I don't know if you're too comfortable or just lazy."

"Both." Her hair disheveled, her face scrubbed, she looked like a teenager in the oversize T-shirt. He checked an urge to peel it from her. "Read the box scores."

"I don't like basketball."

"Bowling?"

She raised only her eyes. "No."

"Tennis?"

Kelly shook her head. From what she gathered, they weren't scoring high at common interests.

"So you don't like basketball, bowling or tennis." He motioned to the book on her coffee table. "But you like time-travel books?"

Kelly decided to settle this. "Yes. We aren't doing well, are we?"

"Sure, we are. I like time-travel stories. I don't bowl or play tennis." He nuzzled her neck. "And I'm crazy about you."

"Well, that's important, isn't it?"

"Everything else be damned," he murmured against her ear, and tossed the newspaper aside.

Except to open the door for a pizza delivery, they never moved off the sofa the whole day. She couldn't recall ever spending a full day doing absolutely nothing. She didn't count the crossword puzzle they worked on while sitting on the sofa and sharing an orange. Or the "Twilight Zone" marathon they'd watched on television.

While she wasn't discontent lazing around, she felt compelled to accomplish something constructive. As night closed in on her apartment, Kelly pushed away from the crook of Denver's arm. It was too late to go into the office, but if she could nudge Denver to move, it might be the right time to see why her sister was so fascinated with Johnny Bellows. "You know where Cowpunchers is, don't you?"

For the past half hour, he'd sensed a restlessness growing in her. He guessed this was one of those big differences between them. He'd learned early in life to relax when he could. He doubted she ever had. "Good country music." He rattled off an address and leaned forward to pick up the last slice of cold pizza from the coffee table. "Why?"

"I'm going to Cowpunchers," she said, disappearing into the bedroom.

Denver straightened. "You aren't going there alone."

A few minutes later, a brush in hand, she reappeared dressed. "If you come along, you'll have to get up."

"I'm up," he said on a huff as he tugged on his boots.

Raindrops plopped in a steady syncopated beat while a famous Tammy Wynette song drifted into the parking lot from the opened doors of the Western dance hall. Couples grouped outside under the overhang of a huge rustic building.

Inside, the bar was dimly lit except over the dance floor where overhead colored lights spotlighted the dancing couples. Kelly threaded her way past the men lining the mahogany bar, leering at every female who passed by. This was definitely an experience she could have lived without.

Following her, Denver was stalled by a gushing redhead.

"You really were wonderful the other day."

Her adulation did nothing for him. He kept walking, trailing Kelly. Her back straight, her head high, she moved through the crowd of men with the dignity and aloofness of royalty.

Feeling thoroughly weighed and measured, Kelly gritted her teeth and scanned the dance floor for her sister.

"Is your sister here?"

She looked over her shoulder at Denver, comfortable with the protectiveness of his hand on her waist. "I haven't found her yet." She glanced away toward the stage and the dark-haired, bearded guitarist. "You never told me what you thought about Johnny Bellows."

A man used to taking, Denver mused, but kept the thought to himself. "Isn't that your sister?" he asked, eyeing a woman who resembled the one from the photograph he'd seen in Kelly's apartment.

Her eyes skimmed the crowd to Jamie seated at one of the long, dark-stained pine tables. As if radar had taken over, Jamie's eyes met hers. Surprise registered first.

Beaming, Jamie wiggled her way past the others at her table and glided toward Kelly. She smiled broadly, her eyes flirtatious. "Wow. This is something. My sister with Denver Casey. You were great."

"Thanks." Sensing they needed time alone, he touched Kelly's shoulder. "I see a friend over at the bar. I'll be right back."

"I can't believe it." Her sister swung a bright-eyed look at her. "You really are going out with Denver Casey?" Jamie dropped to a chair and hunched forward. "How did you do that?" she asked enthusiastically.

"I don't want to talk about me." Kelly sank to the chair beside hers. "Aunt Jean—"

Jamie sighed exaggeratedly. "Oh, let's not do this. I know what you're going to say. Aunt Jean told you I withdrew from my classes."

On the stage, the lead singer was wailing out the last notes of a fast-paced Cajun song. The noise deafening, Kelly leaned closer, straining to talk to her sister. "Yes, she told me. Why would you do that?"

"Because I won't be here."

Kelly was sure she'd misunderstood. "You won't what?"

"I won't be here. Johnny wants me to go with him."

"Go with..." Flabbergasted, Kelly couldn't find words to counter her.

"I think it'll be exciting."

"What will be?" Her heart beating faster, she fought not to yell. "Traveling from one town to the next, never having a place to call home? And for how long?"

Jamie shrugged in a manner that assured Kelly her sister hadn't thought beyond this moment.

"Why are you doing this?" She appealed to reason. "You hardly know him, Jamie. Why would you give up everything, your friends and family, for a man you don't know?"

"I know him well enough, and he'll take me places," she said in an airy tone.

Kelly released a mirthless, disbelieving laugh. "He'll take you to God knows where. And you'll sit around waiting to go to the next place he wants to go."

Her sister's face darkened with anger. "What's so wrong with wanting to see different places?"

"What about a home?"

"You want a home," she shouted as all chance of a quiet, reasonable conversation vanished. "I don't."

"Jamie, please think about this." As her sister started to rise, Kelly grabbed her hand. "You have a choice."

"I've made it," she said defiantly.

"He'll use you. He isn't serious. He'll take you with him and then—"

"I have a right to lead my own life." Her chin lifted, making her look like a petulant child. She snatched her hand free of Kelly's and bounded to a stand. "I'm *going*."

Kelly reached out to stop her and couldn't. Her sister scurried toward Bellows. Stepping off the stage, he touched the hair of an adoring fan before joining Jamie. She stepped into his arms with the trust of a child.

She was in a world of her own, a world that Kelly was no part of. At one time, all either of them had was each other. Feeling as if a piece of herself had just been torn away, she bolted from the chair and tore through the crowd toward the exit.

Almost punishingly, the wind whipped rain at her face. Chilled, she stood for a second, hugging herself. Then someone's arm curled around her shoulder. A touch was all it took. Emotions tightening her chest threatened. Blinking against the rain, she sagged against Denver. "She wouldn't listen," she said with disbelief. "How can she want to traipse around the country and face an uncertain future?"

He wasn't a man who'd comforted many women, but for the first time in his life, he wished by touch to steal away the anguish filling this woman. He didn't doubt that the sisters would mend their differences, but something had been lost tonight for Kelly. He wanted to make these moments easier, but words failed him.

Her throat raw from swallowing against the knot in it, she couldn't speak. No words were needed between them. He held her tight as if trying to draw the frustration and hurt from her. Unmindful of the rain, he kept holding her. She didn't want to lean on any-one. She'd be weaker, she thought as she moved with him toward his truck. But oddly, she felt stronger.

By the time she had inserted her key into the door of her apartment, she'd worked through a dozen emotions. She'd remember the anger between her and Jamie, the harsh words that had passed between them. She'd also never forget that he'd been near when she'd needed him. He'd offered her a friend's solace. He'd given her the strength she'd never expected to find from another.

"Kelly."

"I'm all right," she assured him, meeting his stare with a wry smile. "I wasn't prepared for any of that with her. I..." As he opened the door for her, she couldn't move.

Even beneath the darkness, Denver deciphered the disarray. He stepped in front of her and switched on the light. Cushions had been tossed and slashed. Lamps overturned and broken. Red paint had been dribbled down the center of the carpet. "Stay here."

Her heart pounding as if it would burst through her chest, she nodded obediently.

With caution, he strolled from room to room, checking each one. There was no doubt in his mind who'd broken in or why. Scare the witnesses, and there would be no trial.

Her keys clutched in her hand, Kelly waited at the door, tense, listening until he reappeared.

"They only did the one room." The words sounded stupid to his own ears and offered little consolation.

Kelly heard him but couldn't drag her gaze away from the destruction. Fear only brushed the surface of what she felt. Anger, deep and hot, rushed through her.

The sound of Denver's voice snapped her out of a dazed state. Stunned, she moved to perch on the arm of the sofa while he talked on the phone to the police.

"They'll be here in a few minutes," he said, setting down the receiver. What if he hadn't come in with her? "No argument." He gathered her close. "I'm staying tonight."

For the second time in an hour, she welcomed his embrace. "Who's arguing?" she murmured against his cheek.

Chapter Nine

He awoke, searching the bed for her even before he opened his eyes. Only the sweet scent of her lingered. For a long moment, he listened to rain softly tapping at the window. Anxiety coiled a tight knot in him as he remembered the mess in her living room. He'd spent the night with her, but what about tonight? Or the next night?

While he dressed, he considered a plan. It was fully formed by the time he wandered into the kitchen. He expected to find her. Instead, he found a neatly written message. Swearing, he crinkled her note and didn't bother with the cup of coffee she'd left him. Did she really think after the last two nights that she could get rid of him so easily?

Annoyed, frustrated and worried, he snatched up his hat and stormed toward the door. An image of the chaos in her apartment stayed with him as he jumped into his truck. One destination in mind, he drove to the police station.

"Both brothers made bail yesterday morning," the detective said with an apologetic look.

"Both? I didn't know you'd arrested the gunman."

"One of the witnesses identified him for us."

He knew which one. With an oath, he spun around. Whether she liked it or not, he planned to glue himself to Kelly's side.

Kelly tried to play catch up for yesterday. Work wasn't going well. The police had taken fingerprints but weren't optimistic about finding anything incriminating against the brothers. Kelly never doubted they were the ones intent on making her too frightened to testify. Well, she was no coward.

That wasn't really true. She'd left her apartment early. A coward's way, she knew. But she'd wanted to avoid the awkwardness of a goodbye. Logically, she couldn't make too much of the time they'd shared, no matter how special it had been to her. She wouldn't allow herself to fall under the spell of girlish romantic dreams and assume there'd be more. She didn't ever want to cling to that hope again.

"You look deep in thought."

Startled, she swung around. *About you,* she mused, warming at the sight of him. *Dear God,* she realized, she wanted to rush to him, feel his embrace.

With his shoulder, Denver pushed away from the doorjamb. He'd been so damn tired earlier. Why was it that the sight of her smile drained away fatigue? He stopped at the edge of her desk and sat on it. He'd come with two goals in mind. One centered around reasoning with her, making her see the danger she was in. "I talked to the police this morning. Someone doesn't come in and trash your home for fun. You know that last night wasn't a prank."

Any answer she planned remained unsaid as her aunt swept from the doorway into Kelly's office. "Something happened you didn't tell me about?" she asked in a higher than usual pitch.

Sighing, Kelly prepared herself for an inquisition. With her aunt seated in the chair in front of her, she reassuringly gave her a low-key explanation about last night's incident.

Her efforts were futile. "They did it because you were the one who identified the gunman in the lineup," Jean insisted.

Though more apprehensive than she wanted to admit, even to herself, Kelly forced a weak smile. "Everything will be fine as soon as they go to trial."

"The police should offer you protection."

"They don't need to." Kelly attempted to soothe her. "The gunman is in jail."

Though worrying her aunt wasn't Denver's intent, he'd be damned if he'd let her believe no danger existed. "He made bail. So did his brother."

Distressed, Jean looked from Denver to Kelly. "You can't make light of this, Kelly. You could be in real danger."

"I know a way she won't be," Denver cut in. "She could come with me."

Kelly's head snapped up.

"Where? Your ranch?" Jean asked. "You'd let her stay at the ranch and see your home and talk to you and—"

Aware he had an ally, Denver laughed. "All of that."

Kelly wasn't so inclined. Baffled, she could hardly breathe. He was inviting her into his world. For the sake of the interview, she should be thrilled. Instead, she felt pure panic.

She saw her aunt opening her mouth to accept. She snagged Jean's hand, signaling her to say nothing. "I can't leave. I'm in the middle of another story."

"Kelly, you have to go somewhere until the trial," her aunt insisted. "You've already received threats. You never know what those hoodlums will do."

If only everything her aunt was saying didn't make so much sense. But wasn't everything already out of hand between her and Denver? If she went with him, she might face a different kind of threat. It wasn't that logic had left her. She knew he was giving her an opportunity he hadn't offered to any other reporter, but she couldn't go. "I don't need to go to finish the story."

Denver nearly grabbed her. The offer wasn't made to the reporter, and she knew that. Running. She was still running from him, he realized.

Avoiding his eyes, she nudged back the cuff of her blouse and glanced at her watch. "In fact, I'm late for an appointment." She rounded her desk and darted toward the door before she changed her mind. "Have a safe trip home." She rushed from her office. She'd been so glad to see him. And so close. So close to saying yes to him.

Denver stormed from the building as another downpour began. There was no point in staying any longer. He hit the door of the truck without a word to Dooley. Damn stubborn female. She was hell-bent on standing alone. If she wouldn't leave with him, he couldn't protect her.

He shifted gears with more force than necessary. He handled criticism, others' anger, even enjoyed a difference of opinion with someone. But rejection? It cut him like a knife. Yet, even expecting it from her, he'd taken a chance.

He zipped the truck onto the freeway and stared at the road with its endless white line. It wasn't that he'd wanted to stay in the city. He longed for the country, the smell of hay, the sound of bawling cattle. He simply hadn't been ready to leave without her.

Playing the moonstruck fool didn't sit well with him. Shifting, he felt his kneecap throb. The aches would heal. When he was back at the ranch, he'd forget all the years that he'd ridden hurting from the last rodeo. But miles from her, would he still feel the same longing for her?

As the rain intensified and the windshield wipers swished ineffectually, he slowed the truck. Inside the truck's cab, annoyingly, Dooley whistled a tune about a broken heart. Denver's killing look silenced him.

This wasn't going to work. He wasn't past the city limits, and he couldn't think about anything but her. Rejection be damned. He whipped the truck toward an off ramp.

Dooley swiveled his head from the highway sign to him. "What are you doing?"

Denver wheeled the truck to the on ramp and aimed it for the city. "Going back."

He dropped a smirking Dooley off at a motel and drove to her apartment. Before he left, he'd talk some sense into her.

Kelly arrived home, feeling lousy. Venting her irritability on the disarray in her living room, she tossed the slashed cushions back onto the sofa. She spent ten minutes jamming the stuffing from the cushions into a large garbage bag. Keeping busy wasn't helping. She missed him. He'd been gone only a while, and she already missed him.

More tense than she realized, she jumped when the doorbell rang. "Who's there?"

"A four-time winner and one-time loser."

Kelly fumbled with the chain on the door. "Denver?"

"Let me in. I'm wet. It's cold and—"

She flung the door open.

Grinning, he held a bag out to her. "And I brought you dinner."

Instinctively, she touched his arm. What she wanted to do now was step into his arms. "You didn't leave?"

Low on patience, he stifled the pride damaged by her rejection. "I couldn't," he said quietly.

She reached out to him, coiling her arms around his neck. "I'm glad you didn't leave yet."

They were words he wanted to hold on to. He drew back before he forgot why he was really there. Wants and needs weren't important at the moment. Before he'd leave the city, she'd be with him. "I never asked. Do you like Chinese food?"

She laughed, finding it difficult to release her hold on him. "I love Chinese food." As she hurried ahead of him into the kitchen, words she'd said earlier burdened her. "About what happened in the office . . ."

"I should have known you'd be too busy to leave."

Kelly swiveled a look back at him and wondered what he was up to. The Denver Casey she knew didn't accept defeat easily.

He leaned around her to reach into the silverware drawer. "Did the police find their fingerprints?"

A little guarded, she followed him to the sofa with its deflated cushions. "They haven't called me yet." She kept waiting for him to push, or as he insisted, nudge her to go with him. Instead, as if they'd skipped that scene in her office, they shared again easy conversation that mingled with laughter and smiles. Grinning at his comment about Dooley's proclivity for rocky-road ice cream, Kelly offered him a fortune cookie. "Is he as much of a chocaholic as I am?"

"No one is," Denver gibed. He motioned to the slip of paper in her hand. "What does it say?"

"Everything is all right."

Denver sent her a skeptical look. "Let me see."

Laughing, she drew back her hand to dodge his. "Don't you believe me?"

"No." He lunged, tumbling with her back on her chair. Pinning her, he snatched the slip of paper from her hand. "It says..." He paused and met her eyes. "Listen to a friend."

Trapped beneath him, she laughed. "I knew you'd take it personally."

"Damn straight."

She dodged the seriousness she heard in his voice. "What does yours say?"

"You'll get what you want." His eyes held hers. "Will I?"

"What do you want?" she asked lightly.

His eyes carried no humor. "I want you to come with me." He lowered his head until only inches separated their faces. "It's not safe for you here."

Didn't he know that there was more danger for her in going with him than staying? She might be safe from the robbers' threats. But how would she protect her heart?

"Until the trial," he added quickly, sensing she needed some time limit.

"If I go with..." She paused, a fire kindling as his hand snaked under her blouse. "If I go with you, we'll get closer and—"

"How close?" he asked against her collarbone.

She sensed the danger of love sneaking up on her. "Close."

"But you'll be safer."

"Will I be?"

"I'll never let you out of my sight."

She shivered, her nipple hardening with the gentle stroke of his finger. "You'll do more of that, won't you?" she asked breathlessly.

"Much more."

With three suitcases jammed in the back of her rental car, Kelly insisted he make one stop before they left the city.

There were a dozen places he'd rather be than her office. Denver took a swipe at the strings of the deflating balloons and jammed his hands into the back pockets of his worn jeans.

"Won't Dooley be looking for you?" Kelly frowned into a drawer. Why was she having such difficulty organizing everything? She usually had an orderly mind.

"I already called him. He's taking the truck and the horse trailer. We'll have to use that swanky rental car of yours." He strolled to the window. "Okay?"

"That's fine."

Denver looked out the window. The rain was a faint mist now, but a gray sky still hid the tops of the skyscrapers. Even on warm days, the city looked cold to him. At home, clouds floated over the peaks of mountains as if playing hide-and-seek with them, yet the color of the land, vivid greens and browns, treated the eye. To him, there was no gray at the ranch. No coldness. As her telephone rang, he glanced back at her, growing impatient to leave her office, and the city. "Don't answer it."

Kelly sent him a look of disbelief. "I have to. One more minute," she promised.

He looked at his watch to time her, drawing her laugh. How the hell could she function so normally when he felt so baffled by feelings for her?

"That was my realtor," she said exuberantly as she set down the receiver. "The seller is weakening."

His gut tightened that they weren't even gone and she was already making plans for her return to the city.

"I heard you were here. I thought—" Jean took two steps in and halted, her attention shifting to Denver lounging against the windowsill.

He tipped his hat. "I'm here under duress," he said lightly. "She's a workaholic, isn't she?"

"Oh, yes, I'm afraid so."

Kelly stilled in gathering work. "I'm going to the ranch," she explained.

"Thank goodness, you'll be safe."

Her aunt sounded so certain, Kelly mused.

"When are you leaving?"

"Soon." Kelly reclosed her desk file drawer. "But I wanted to take some work with me."

"Take some time to smell the flowers," her aunt advised.

What choice would she have? With no schedules to meet, no computer nearby, she'd be on a forced vacation. As her aunt gave her a quick goodbye hug, Kelly couldn't help asking, "Did you see Jamie this morning?"

Jean heaved a sigh. "She's already left."

Denver watched the worried exchange and pushed away from the window. "Where's the vending machine?"

"Coffee's terrible here," Kelly warned him.

Casually he stroked her hand in passing. "I'll take my chances." He'd taken a lot of them in his life, but never one this big.

"What did she say?" Kelly asked when the door closed behind him.

"She's worried you're angry at her."

"I am." A rush of irritation returned as she recalled her sister's attitude last night. "She wouldn't listen to anything I said."

Jean raised her hands in an appeal. "Kelly, don't—"

"Don't what?" It was so much easier to go with the anger than the hurt.

Her eyebrows knitting, Jean shook her head. "It's so easy to turn away. But none of us understood what your mother must have felt. She was a woman alone with a child to raise. Your grandparents were angry, too, when your mother said she was leaving with Ray. They lived to regret it. Your grandfather said some harsh words to her. Unforgivable words."

Strain crept into her voice. "We didn't hear from your mother again." She slipped off her glasses and kneaded her forehead as if suddenly pained. "If we'd been less estranged, I would have known she needed help, been there sooner for you and Jamie. You wouldn't have spent all that time with social services and in foster homes."

"None of that was your fault."

"I'm not blameless."

"Why are you telling me this?"

"Kelly, you've always taught Jamie to know what she wants. Now, she wants to make her own decisions, make her own mistakes, live her own life."

Be her own person. It seemed Jamie had heard her. How many times had she said just that to her?

"We have to be here for her if she needs us," Jean insisted softly.

So wise, Kelly mused. Would she ever emulate this woman who seemed to possess so much confidence, so much compassion, such ability to see beyond the moment?

"I'd never forgive myself if Jamie thought she couldn't come home if she learns she was wrong, would you?" her aunt asked.

A heavy pressure, very real and physical, filled her chest. How difficult it must be for a parent to watch their child making a mistake! She felt the same anxiety for her sister. She was so young and so unprepared for the heartache. "No, I wouldn't."

Jean smiled and hugged her again. "You'll call often," she insisted.

"Often," Kelly promised.

Denver stilled in the doorway. Alone, her head bent, Kelly closed a briefcase. Because concern still shadowed her eyes, he didn't believe the smile she offered him.

"I'm ready."

"Your sister didn't return home?" At the shake of her head, he joined her at the window. The look of despair in her eyes spoke volumes. "Because she went with him, do you think she's forgotten what you told her?"

"Yes—no." Her voice sounded too loud. She looked away from the blue eyes studying her. What could he see when she wasn't even sure what she was feeling? She only knew she had to accept that she couldn't protect Jamie any longer. Her sister would make her own choices now, some good, some bad.

His hand on hers, he watched her back straighten. He'd never met any woman with her determination to stand on her own. She knew how to hang tough. He doubted she'd appreciate knowing that was one trait essential for any woman living on a ranch.

"This is so dumb." She sighed. "I feel so far from her. I feel..." She paused and looked at him.

"Your sister will come around," he said softly.

"Are you always this optimistic?"

"You could drive yourself crazy worrying about what you can't change."

Kelly worked up a genuine smile. "Can I quote you?"

Because he knew how much she needed lightness at the moment, he laughed. "If you must."

She felt tension easing from her. "On this ranch of yours, do you have a hammock?"

Perched on the edge of the windowsill, he cocked an eyebrow suggestively. "Yeah, I do. Do you like hammocks?"

"I knew it. You look like a hammock man." How did he ease her troubled mind so easily? she wondered. The answer didn't really matter. She gave in to the feelings that had nagged at her since she'd entered the office. She stepped into the space between his legs and draped an arm over his shoulder. "And I bet you just sack out there every chance you get."

Grinning, he tugged her close. "There's room for two on that hammock."

"I'd go crazy doing nothing."

His fingers skimmed her hip. "Oh, there's always something to do."

On a laugh, she nudged him affectionately with her elbow, then sidestepped the hand caressing her thigh. "I'll be back in a minute."

"Where are you going?"

"To get a camera—unless you'll let one of the magazine photographers come along."

"Get the camera," he practically growled, ready to kick himself for agreeing to this. He wanted her near, needed to see her at the ranch. The woman, not the reporter. Only they were one and the same, something he couldn't allow himself to forget. For his father's sake, he'd be cautious. To the woman, he'd give everything. To the reporter, he'd give as much as he could without hurting another person.

Nothing was as she'd expected. She'd planned to make the best of this trip, so sure she'd feel isolation, hate everything. But he didn't live in some hovel in the middle of the wilderness. Instead of weathered-looking buildings in the middle of a dusty prairie, she saw a crisp white two-story ranch house with Wedgwood blue shutters. White fencing surrounded the ranch buildings, while the house, flanked by silver-trunked aspens, had a white picket fence. And a garden. Her eyes fixed on the garden alive with colorful blossoms. She'd dreamed of a garden like that.

She stepped from the car, surrounded by sound. From the huge trees bordering the driveway came the chirp of birds. Men perched on the rails of a far-off corral and yelled encouragement to a ranch hand skirting a wide berth around a skittish horse. Two Border collies raced to greet Denver.

Laughing, he crouched down to ruffle their fur.

"Quite a welcoming committee." Kelly touched his shoulder, then reached down to pet one of the dogs.

Denver swept a look over the house, the land. It felt good to be home. "Come on." Eager to step inside, he linked his hand with hers and drew her along with him.

It was a man's home. Rustic with lots of leather and comfortable furniture and Western art. But the room he showed her on the second floor carried an air of femininity from the tiny print in the wallpaper to the white quilt. Admiringly Kelly stroked the brass headboard and feasted her eyes on the oil lamp and an antique pitcher and bowl on a mahogany table.

"Is it okay?"

She realized that was the first time she'd ever heard him uncertain about anything. Stepping into his arms, she gave him a reassurance. "It's lovely. I didn't expect anything like this."

Pleasurably he fingered a strand of her silky hair. With her face tilted toward him, her breath mingled with his. Warm and tempting, it made fatigue from the drive drift away. A twist of the lock on the door, he thought, and he could nudge her back onto the soft bed.

She traced the deep smiling groove near the corner of his mouth. All she had to do was look into his eyes to know where his thoughts had strayed. "Don't you have to go downstairs? Your father—" She paused as a man appeared in the doorway.

A ghost of a smile touched his deep-set eyes. "Heard you were home."

With a look over his shoulder, Denver made an introduction. "My father."

She felt a little flutter of nerves. She'd known his home, the land he loved, would stir memories for her, some she'd like to forget forever. But a different kind of tension moved through her. Self-conscious, Kelly eased out of his embrace and offered her hand. "Mr. Casey."

"Will," he corrected. For a brief second, guardedness flickered in his dark, alert eyes. "The only person who calls me Mr. Casey is my accountant." The essence of the old-time cowboy, a man with a thatch of gray hair, he was tall, broad and weathered looking. Firmly he took her hand as if measuring her by her handshake. "Nice to have you here. And you," he said, giving his son a welcome hug. "Damn good to have you home."

"Same here."

He patted Denver's shoulder. "Come downstairs, now."

As he stepped from the room, Denver chuckled. "Dinner must be ready." He wrapped an arm around her shoulder. "Come on, before the bear starts growling."

"His moods are controlled by his stomach?"

He didn't need to answer. They reached the top of the staircase and knew the reason for his father's abruptness.

A houseful of people greeted them.

The buzz of voices, the robust sounds of laughter mingled together. Women hugged Denver. Men slapped his back and pumped his hand. Names, most of which Kelly doubted she'd remember, floated around her. They'd come not to hobnob with a world champion but to welcome home one of their own.

Her hand tucked in his, Kelly stood close beside him, not unaware of curious or speculative stares, and listened to a neighbor tell Denver he'd missed the flood of the century.

"It'll make good grazing land," Will said. "We need something in our favor. What with the fluctuating price of beef," he grumbled. "Damn up and down. Can't predict cattle 'futures.' Everything depends on marketing and grazing fees."

Everything had depended on the land for her stepfather, too, Kelly reflected. Ray's family's well-being had been at the mercy of a pump digging low enough to find oil. If not, he was out of work and they were on the move again in search of another pump, another job.

"Want to get something to eat?" Denver asked.

Nodding, Kelly looked away from studying Will's profile. Perhaps Denver had the same stubborn, square jaw, but she knew now the high cheekbones, the blue of his eyes, even his smile were from his mother.

A step from the table, Denver was enveloped in the arms of a small, portly woman with white hair. Keeping an arm around her ample waist, he turned her toward Kelly. "Lorna Barnes." He grinned down at her. "Best cook in these parts."

"Oh, quit buttering me up," she reprimanded, but looked pleased.

"Can I help?" Kelly asked, gesturing toward the basket of freshly baked breads and rolls Lorna had just set on the table.

"No, you just enjoy yourself." She beamed at Kelly. "I knew Denver wouldn't bring home some la-di-da woman."

Kelly paused in reaching for a potato chip. "La-di-da?"

Chuckling, Denver glanced away and caught his father's signal. "I'll be back."

Lorna's smile widened. "Talk spreads real quick around here. Everyone was saying Denver had himself a classy lady. That you are. But I didn't reckon you'd be one of those kinds who'd worry about messing her nail polish or expect to be waited on like some queen. Denver wouldn't abide by a woman who took to pampering like some women do."

Smiling, Kelly picked up a plate for the buffet. "Have you been here long?"

"Nearly twenty years." Lorna set a spoon in one bowl. "We owned a small place of our own adjoining the Circle C. We sold it to the Caseys, and my husband semiretired. Charlie." She looked around the room. "Well, he's here somewhere. Anyway, he couldn't stand it, so we came over here. That was about the time that Mary Ellen—"

Kelly angled a look at her. The woman's lips were pressed so tight suddenly that they looked pinched. Loyalty was so rare to see, Kelly mused. But didn't she owe her aunt the best job she could do? "Mary Ellen was Denver's mother?"

"She was," she said with a glance at Denver.

"He mentioned that she liked the city."

The woman swept a look over the table as if it were the first time she'd seen the food. "She was used to a different life." With a look of deep concentration, she shifted several bowls. "So they needed someone for the kitchen," she said, taking the conversation back. "And Charlie hired on as their cow boss."

Across the room, Denver noted Lorna's distressed look in his direction. He was torn between it and the network of frown lines wrinkling his father's forehead. "She's a looker."

"Yeah, that she is."

Will contemplated him with an expression that used to make Denver squirm. "She's just visiting?"

"I don't know." Not wanting to dull his own good spirits, he steered conversation down a more companionable path. "Tell me what's been happening around here," he said, moving toward Kelly.

His father did as expected and walked with him. "Got plenty for you to do."

Denver reached Kelly and touched the back of her neck. "Bet there's a pile of bookkeeping," he razzed his father.

"I kept the books up-to-date." Will chuckled self-deprecatingly. "Sort of. But you're going to be busy. Think you can handle it?"

Denver took his father's goading tone in stride. "I didn't get that soft."

"There's a fence to repair, the windmill is out at section eight and—"

Denver raised a halting hand. "I get the picture. I'll be busy until next March."

Kelly tilted her head, confused by words that sounded as if he'd be staying here for a long while. "Don't you have another rodeo to compete in?"

"I'll be staying."

"Staying?"

At the bewilderment knitting her eyebrows, he smiled. "That's a scoop. Phoenix was my last rodeo. I'm settling down."

During the past hour, she realized she'd given the interview little thought. Now, every inquisitive bone in her body was on alert again. "Why?"

He wondered if the question had come from the woman he'd made love to or the reporter hungry for a story. "A smart rodeo man gets out before he breaks one bone too many. Namely his neck."

But he didn't have to be here. He was famous. People wanted him to do endorsements. Even Hollywood might be interested. Kelly spoke her thoughts. "And you're staying here?"

He didn't understand why she was questioning that. "It's where I belong."

The simplicity of his answer was a stark reminder of the different world he yearned for. He hadn't even been willing to give up this life for his mother, she reminded herself.

"What's this business about a scoop?" Will asked, frowning.

Kelly turned a smile on him. "I'm a reporter. That's how I met Denver. I'm writing a story about him."

As if a cloud had dropped over him, Will's face darkened. "A reporter."

Only an idiot wouldn't have noticed that his tone carried no admiration.

"Can't imagine what you could find so interesting to write about him," he said in a feigned light tone that Kelly didn't buy.

She felt as if the welcome mat had been whisked out from under her. Only one reason made sense to her. Secrets. They had secrets.

As Denver became an unwilling audience to a neighbor's tirade about cattle prices, Kelly found herself a captive one to a woman who'd been his first-grade teacher.

The evening wore down. No one talked about the latest fashion trends or the symphony or the opening of a new art gallery. Yet, she found herself laughing and listening with interest, and not missing any of her usual topics of conversation.

With an arm around Denver's waist, she stood next to him on the porch and watched the last car pull away.

Turning her toward the house, he winked. "Ready for bed?"

"You're so subtle," she said on a laugh. "What about your father?"

Lazily he kissed her jaw. "He sleeps soundly."

Chapter Ten

Kelly expected early-morning wake-ups but four a.m. was the middle of the night in a civilized world. She peeked from behind sleepy lids into a room mantled by darkness.

Beside her, his warm leg brushing against her, Denver muttered a soft oath, then groped around for the alarm clock.

Fortunately the ringing of the alarm stopped. "What time is it?" she murmured.

Moaning, he tossed back covers and pushed himself to the edge of the mattress. His back felt as if someone had walked across it all night, his left leg ached to straighten and his shoulder burned. Some rodeo injuries haunted a man forever. "Too early for you," he responded softly to her. "Go back to sleep." At the brush of her fingers on his back, he fought his way back from falling under the spell of a dream.

Kelly giggled. "You were nearly snoring sitting up." Lightly she nipped his shoulder. "Come back here."

"I have to get up." He wasn't sure if he was saying the words for her benefit or his own, but he fell back on the bed beside her.

"Not now," she murmured, reaching for him. Need, not want. That's what she was feeling. Need was so much more complicated.

His face in her hair, he was already lost in the softness of her. As the taste of her filled his mouth, he touched what was familiar to him now. But each time it was as if it were the first time. The warmth of her kiss, the caress of her hands, the meeting of their bodies drove him.

The dreamy state of morning slipped away. With her arms and legs around him, he tasted a wild insistence in the mouth on his. Urgency rushing over them, he tumbled her with him, tangling his hand in her hair. Dark eyes, hooded with passion, stared up at him. He wanted her no less now than any other time. Each time, need and want blended more. Each time, sensation intensified. Pleasure, torment, they melded. Their hearts beating faster, their breaths coming quicker, they began a journey that would weaken and strengthen him.

Sunlight streamed into the room, its warmth shrouding them, but a different heat was already bathing them, making the flesh beneath his hands slick with passion. He molded, then gripped her to him. From outside, he heard sounds as familiar to him as they were when he was a boy. Nothing had changed. Everything had, he realized as he entered her, as she arched to meet him.

Lazy and warm, Kelly roused herself slowly from sleep. It was past eight when she finally showered and dressed. Instead of the abrasive beeping of car horns, the pleasant sound of birds chirped outside her window. When was the last time she'd stayed in bed past seven o'clock, when her mind didn't immediately rush to the problems of an assignment, when she hadn't let time rule her life? she wondered.

She made a concession to light makeup, dabbing on blusher and mascara. After brushing her hair, she ambled down the steps. Big. The house was so much bigger than she'd thought.

Seeing no one, she roamed toward what she thought was the kitchen. In the center of it was a weathered worktable. Blue-and-white gingham cushions complemented the rough-hewn furniture.

Her hands coated with flour, Lorna offered a bright welcome. "Good morning."

"Morning. I suppose everyone else has been up a long time."

"Four-thirty is breakfast." At Kelly's groan, Lorna laughed and snatched up a towel to wipe off her hands. "Now, you sit down." She set a coffee cup on the table. "And I'll get you some juice and then fry you up a couple of eggs and—"

Kelly raised a halting hand. "Just the coffee and juice."

She gave Kelly a reprimanding stare that was maternal. "Got to have more than that."

"Toast." Kelly gestured toward the bowl of flour. "I'll get the juice. You're busy."

Not expecting to see Denver until lunch, she explored the house after breakfast. Half an hour later, she concluded it might take days to see everything. Wandering down a hallway lined with Western art, she paused outside double doors. The soft clicking of a keyboard roused her curiosity, and she quietly opened the doors. Sitting behind a desk, he was hunched over a stack of papers, his fingers flying across a computer keyboard.

He looked different. His boots kicked off, with one stockinged foot he tapped in time with the banjo music coming from a stereo. Smiling, she tiptoed up behind him and slipped her arms around his neck. "You have many talents," she murmured, kissing the curve of his neck.

His voice carried a laugh. "I thought you already knew that."

Beneath her hands, his body relaxed, muscles softening. "Yes, but I couldn't include those in my article." She scanned the columns of numbers. "When did you learn to do this?"

Leaning back, he tilted his head up for a kiss. "At college."

She wondered what else he'd never told her. With envy, she eyed the computer, the beautiful printer. To a writer, it was like finding a piece of home. "Didn't you say you were going to help with the fencing today?"

A wry grin curling the edges of his lips, he took her hand and drew her around the chair and down to his lap. "I'd prefer to be out there, but I'm playing catch-up."

She coiled an arm around his neck but still eyed the monitor. "I could do this for you."

"Why would you want to?" he asked distractedly, more interested in the curve of her neck.

"A favor for a favor."

Slowly his lips trailed down to the quickening beat of her pulse. "Ah."

She felt his smile against her flesh.

"You want to use the computer," he said rather than asked.

"The laptop is okay. But you have a printer and..." Her voice trailed off as he nibbled at her collarbone.

"Convince me," he murmured.

An hour later, Denver ambled outside. He couldn't stop smiling. Romance. It wasn't something he'd ever looked for. He'd had his share of flings, but never had any woman filled his mind constantly.

He'd wanted to see her at the ranch, but by nature he was more of a realist than a dreamer. Though he'd offered her a safe haven, he never forgot that she'd feel compelled to pick his life apart. He'd worked too hard to let anyone do that to him or his father. The problem was he suddenly couldn't imagine a day without her. But to love her, really love her, he'd have to trust her.

He stopped at the well and dipped the cup into the bucket. A midmorning sun disappeared behind a fluffy white cloud. The breeze cooled, ruffling the mane of an ebony colt in a nearby corral.

"He's a restless one," a voice said behind him.

Denver had already caught the scent of his father's pipe tobacco.

Grim, Will lumbered closer as if too many burdens rested on his shoulders. "She's asking questions, Denver. Lorna said she asked about Mary Ellen."

He expected Kelly to probe. She'd spent too many years honing her skills to stop now for him. What he wasn't sure of was what she'd do with the truth if she learned it.

Beneath the brim of his hat, his father's eyes looked fathomless. "She's going to poke into our business."

Because he couldn't deny it, he said nothing. He dropped the cup back into the bucket and fixed his eyes on the colt again. Strolling closer to the corral, he wondered if there'd be a price to pay if he did trust her completely.

Prancing, the colt sought a far corner of the corral. It was spirited, a beautiful animal. He'd break it gently. In the end, it would accept its rider but still have its pride. Pride. Without it, a man was nothing.

By late afternoon, Kelly had finished logging receipts. Before she'd come to the ranch, she'd always thought of ranchers, even Denver, as cowboys. She'd learned that he was a wise businessman, that without the skill of good management, a ranch wouldn't succeed. The ranch had an impressive bookkeeping system, and she gathered from Denver's notations of accountable working hours for each ranch hand that he'd spent hours huddled over the paperwork.

Stacking up the receipts, she noted the tally books needed updating. Tomorrow, she'd record the information into a permanent record. There was a lot more work to do, but she pushed back the worn leather chair, needing fresh air.

From the porch, she saw Denver patting the neck of an ebony-colored colt. Before her exploration of the house, she'd taken photographs that morning of some of the cowhands and had jotted down notes for an indepth story about the American cowboy. She assumed the trial wouldn't begin for weeks. With that kind of time ahead, she needed to keep busy or she'd go crazy.

The wind whipping at her, she bowed her head against the dust whirling in the air. As she neared the rails, she felt the curious stares of several men gathered near. One of them, a deep-creased, tanned cowboy nodded his hat in greeting.

"I'm Kelly," she said as a way of introduction.

"Shucks, I know who you are. I saw you last night at the party." His dark eyes danced with friendliness. "When we heard about Denver's lady, we guessed you might be comin' along. My wife said you're okay. Gettin' an okay from Lorna ain't easy."

Kelly matched his smile. "Oh, you're Charlie."

"Yes, ma'am. I'm the cow boss." He motioned with his head toward Denver who was still coaxing the skittish colt. "It's his first day in a halter." Charlie rested a booted foot on a bottom rail. "Denver believes in makin' friends with the horse. He'll be takin' it slow and easy."

Slow and easy. And with soft words and gentle hands. The same way he made love. She smiled to herself. The colt didn't have a chance.

As shadows lengthened, Kelly roused herself from a lazy mood and strolled toward the house. The air smelled of livestock and leather. The bellowing of cattle drifted on a cool wind as the sun cast an orange glow on the snow-dusted mountain tops. An artist's dream, she mused, viewing the purple clouds and a pink sky.

"Sure is pretty out here, isn't it?" Will said, letting the screen door slam behind him. Instead of moving on, he stopped across from her and leaned against a post. "The land fools a person sometimes. It's not so pretty when a storm comes up." He paused to take out his pipe. "Around here, plenty can happen. A cowpoke can get kicked in the groin by a yearling, or hooked by a horn, or find himself flattened by a horse."

Though he'd spoken in an offhand tone, Kelly assumed he was deliberately choosing to present her with the worst scenarios, make her see the harshness of the land and the weather. She needed no lesson.

Head bent, he lit and puffed on his pipe. "Winter isn't easy. Sometimes the roads get too rough to go into town."

"But we're all still here," Denver drawled from a few feet away. The brim of his hat shading his face, he climbed the steps and gave his father a sharp glance. "Isn't that right?"

Two strong men stood almost eye to eye for a moment, then Will laughed. In that brief instant, Kelly felt the strength and determination of both of them. And a love that was linked by more than blood. They were more than father and son. They were friends.

Shrugging, Will stepped away. "Suppose so," he said without a look back.

Because of Denver's frown, Kelly offered a smile. "Were you looking for me?"

"Always." He caressed her shoulder. "I thought we'd go for a ride before dinner." He tugged her close and searched her face. "If he—"

She inched against him, setting a finger against his lips. "He loves you."

Her understanding pulled at him. She was giving to him without conditions. She might not even be aware of it, but he could feel it happening. And he was still holding back. Uneasy as nerves fluttered in his stomach, he tightened his hold on her. He wondered how it was possible she could make him forget the aches in his knees from squatting too long while shoeing a horse, the tension he felt whenever his father was near her. "He can be difficult."

Kelly felt the edge of tension in him. "I thought you didn't worry about anything."

He pressed his lips to her cheek. "Not what I can't control."

A tease riding her tongue, she turned her face up to him. "Don't you know you can't influence a stubborn man?"

He couldn't help smiling. "You think he's stubborn?"

"It runs in the family, doesn't it?" she said with a soft laugh.

Grasping the humor she'd worked hard to stir, he narrowed his eyes, feigning a threatening look.

Laughing, she slipped out of his arms but laced her fingers through his. "Of course, I happen to know some wonderful, stubborn men."

He arched an eyebrow, drawing her with him toward the stable. "Many?"

Laughing again, she nudged him with an elbow. "One in particular."

The mare he'd picked out for her was a palomino with a light gold color and a snow-white mane and tail. As if offering instant friendship, she nuzzled Kelly's neck.

"Her name's Sunbeam." Denver hoisted a saddle over a bay, a magnificent-looking horse with black legs and a black mane and tail. "Do you know how to—"

She sent him a withering look. "If I ride her, I can saddle her."

He stifled a grin. What had caught his attention from the start was her spirit, sometimes defiant but always determined. He admired the way she thrust out her chin and resisted crumbling beneath threats. A soft woman couldn't survive on a ranch. She'd need stamina, a streak of independence, and plenty of self-assurance to handle whatever problem came along.

Absently she stroked the mare's nose. "You're lost in thought."

Denver wrestled for any excuse. "I was thinking about Dooley."

She didn't believe him. While he didn't look troubled, he seemed preoccupied by something more thought provoking. She supposed secrets were part of their relationship. Without them, wouldn't they get too close? Without them, the narrow distance keeping them from being one would be bridged. "I haven't seen him since we arrived."

"He's in town, visiting a lady friend." He finished tightening the cinch. "We probably won't see him for a month." He laughed softly with private amusement. "When he does come, he'll be ten pounds heavier. Chelsea believes that the way to a man's heart is through his stomach."

Mounting the horse, she glanced around her. There were people in his life she didn't even know. It was best if it stayed that way, she decided.

They rode at a leisurely gait. By the time they returned to the stables, dusk had crept over the land. His arm at her waist, he urged her toward the house. She looked relaxed. For that reason alone, he was glad she'd come. "It's almost dinnertime."

Nodding, she scanned the outbuildings, then laughed, abruptly stopping. "What is that?" She motioned to a nearby tree and the words etched inside a heart on the trunk. "Lynn loves Billy."

"I was only nine."

At the amusement in his eyes, a teasing spirit swept over her. "And precocious."

"She had the crush, not me."

Laughing, she shifted in his embrace to lay her head back on his shoulder. A windmill whistled and creaked. Bright sunflowers peeked up around rocks along a creek, and a herd of white-faced Herefords grazed at the foot of pine-filled mountains, their peaks still dusted by snow. "Irresistible, were you?"

"It's my country charm," he said in a tone that made fun of himself.

Serenity. Almost tangible, its soothing effect was inching its way down her body. "It's really beautiful here."

He splayed a palm over her belly and nuzzled her neck.

"You're not looking, are you?" she asked teasingly.

"I'm seeing what I want to see."

She felt his smile against her skin. "I bet you broke a lot of hearts."

"Millions."

Tilting her head back, she brought her mouth a hairbreadth from his. "So I'm just one more."

"Yep." He turned her around and pulled her close. "One in a million."

Morning light spilled into the barn. During the two days that had passed, a routine had settled in. Denver had worried she'd be bored, but she surprised him again. Whether she realized it or not, she was as at home here as she'd been in the city.

Knowing she liked a morning ride, he strolled into the stable and past stalls until he reached Sunbeam's. For a moment, he stood still, watching her brush each side of the mare. "Been looking for you."

With a smile, Kelly looked back at him. "Sunbeam and I have been bonding."

He laughed. "It's time to bond with me for a while." What still amazed him was that a city girl knew how to groom a horse. "Where did you learn that?"

With care, she used a wet brush to sweep Sunbeam's mane to one side. "At the stable I used to go to outside the city. The horses' owners were adamant about riders learning to care for their horses."

A stream of sunlight caught her hair as she bent forward for the mare's hoof. He felt his heart catch at her intention and stepped forward instinctively. "I'll do that."

Over her shoulder, she sent him an amused look. "I can do it."

Uneasy, he stilled. The protectiveness wasn't new to him. Keeping her safe had motivated him to bring her to his ranch, but he'd seen the results of a horse's kick.

"Look..." he started, then quieted, noting that she'd moved to stand close to the mare's shoulder. Facing toward the rear of the horse, she ran her hand down the horse's leg and squeezed gently. As the mare lifted her foot, she grasped the hoof firmly, and starting at the back of it, she used the hoof pick to remove dirt from the V-shaped area.

Relaxing, Denver settled back against an upright. He couldn't argue with someone who knew what she was doing. As she bent again, denim strained against her thighs. If he closed his eyes, he could pull up the feeling of them, slender and strong, wrapped around him. He nearly laughed out loud at his own thoughts. He had it bad. Real bad. Desire taunting him, he glanced at the nearby mound of hay. "Ever make love in a hayloft?"

Kelly shot a grin at him. "You country boys sure are single-minded."

"Good clean living gives a man healthy ideas."

Amusement edged her voice. "Only you would come up with that answer." She picked up another hoof. "Why were you looking for me?"

"We have to go somewhere."

"Where?"

She swung away from putting the hoof pick back on the shelf to find herself cornered.

His arms bracketing her shoulders, he slanted a look at the nearby hay, then tumbled down with her.

Laughing against his lips, she touched his jaw, aware that she knew the feel of his face now better than her own. "Didn't you say we had to go somewhere?"

"To town." One kiss, and with a swiftness that shocked his system, his blood warmed. It would be so easy to forget everything but her. He realized how often he felt that way now. Poised above her, he took a moment longer to savor the taste of her. What he couldn't do was think too far into the future. "You're driving me crazy," he said with a laugh at himself, then lifted away from her.

Lazily Kelly lingered on the soft bed of hay. "Why aren't you busy today?"

He caught her hand and drew her to a stand with him. "I'm busy," he countered, leaning to the side and brushing hay from her backside.

She smiled as his fingers strayed to the curve of her hip.

"I never get enough of you," he said suddenly on a whisper that fanned her cheek. "All morning I thought about you, about holding you like this."

"Funny—" casually she slid her hand around his neck "—I was thinking the same thing."

"And you said we had nothing in common," he teased.

"Yes." She gave a dramatic sigh. "I was wrong."

"Come on before I change my mind." Grinning, he slid a hand down to her arm and drew her outside with him. Beneath a brisk wind, her hair became tossed, the strands twisting. The feelings he felt for her were just as entangled, he realized. "Here."

In amazement, she stared at the grocery list he'd shoved in her hand. "Twenty-five pounds of flour?"

"That's a small grocery list." Denver opened the truck door for her. "Lorna needed extra for the party."

Kelly looked up from the paper. "A party?"

"Don't ask me." His expression baffled, he shrugged. "Pa's got it in his head to invite the neighbors over for a barbecue at the end of the month."

Why? Kelly wanted to ask. Though she'd grown comfortable with the ranch surroundings, amiable with the cowhands and had quickly become good friends with Lorna, Will still held her at a polite distance. Why would he invite friends over to meet her?

The question lingered during the bumpy ride over a dirt-and-gravel road. Low growing juniper and shaggy shrubs stretched forever. Kelly gazed at a cliff alive with greenery. "When I was young, I'd ride in the back of my family's pickup and hate every moment, every brown blade of grass, every cow I saw. But this is beautiful."

Denver glanced at her. Her arm propped on the edge of the window, she turned her face into the wind, letting it flow over her. She looked content, but her words stirred a disturbing reminder. If it hadn't been for the threats, she wouldn't be here with him. He drove the rest of the way in silence, impatient words too close to slipping out.

Before she saw them, Kelly smelled a hint of the pine bordering the town. It looked as if it had never progressed out of the twentieth century with its plank sidewalks and Western storefronts.

His hand linked with hers, Denver wandered along with her down the street and into stores as if they were teenagers who'd just found each other.

Everywhere Kelly felt friendliness.

In the grocery store, Adele, a second cousin of Denver's, shared gossip and offered cookies. In a craft boutique, the man told her the history of an artist who'd made a carving of a horse that reminded her of Sunbeam, and at a Western apparel shop, the saleswoman talked about a recent horse show while Kelly tried on boots so soft they felt like slippers.

"There's even a dance after the show," the woman added.

Kelly nodded, distracted by Denver's hand kneading her back. As the woman went on, Kelly listened halfheartedly to her, her attention shifting to a shapely redhead in snug jeans.

She strolled into the store, her flashing dark eyes riveted on Denver. Almost simultaneously, he pushed out of a chair as she stepped up to him. Without hesitation, she threw her arms around his neck.

A faint sensation of discomfort, clearly tinged with jealousy, slithered through Kelly. It didn't please her one bit. Jealousy went hand in hand with other deep feelings.

"Finally," the redhead said teasingly.

Kelly stifled her own feelings and plastered a silly grin to her face as the redhead sent her a quick grin before looking back at him.

"I thought you were getting too bigheaded to ever come home," she teased.

"You look—" He paused and drew a deep breath.

She fed him a line. "Terrific?"

"And more, Doc." Turning her with him, he noted the unusual flush coloring Kelly's cheeks. "Kelly, this is Jean Lane. The town's doctor."

"We went to school together," Jean explained.

Facing off with one of his old girlfriends ranked low on Kelly's list of enjoyable things to do.

The redhead sent him a look of affection. "And double-dated. Others," she added quickly with a friendly smile for Kelly. "He was with Sue Ann Kimball."

As Jean made a distasteful face, Kelly felt a genuine laugh slip out.

The warmth of acceptance floated into Jean's voice. "Next time you're in town—" she paused and laughed as she gestured with her thumb at Denver "—dump him. And we'll have lunch and girl talk."

Affectionately he brushed shoulders with her. "You're still a brat, aren't you?"

"Still am," she said with a laugh, then whisked out as quickly as she'd entered.

Kelly gave herself a pat on the back for not letting the green-eyed monster dig its claws into her. "She seems nice."

"One of the best," he said as she preceded him outside. In passing, he nodded at Sybil Newman, the town gossip. Within an hour, she'd have circulated a full description of Kelly to anyone who'd listen.

Kelly looked down and admired her new boots. "Why didn't you date her?"

"She and a buddy had it bad for each other." He curled his hand over hers. "But went their separate ways."

"Why?"

"He was from the wrong side of the tracks," he answered to offer the simplest explanation. "Why all the questions? Jealous?"

She wrinkled her nose, determined to make light of his words and what she'd briefly felt. "No, she's not your type."

Amusement slipped into his voice. "Sure of yourself, aren't you?"

Stopping at the curb, she raised her lips to him. "Kiss me first."

He laughed, drawing her against him. As his mouth slanted across hers, he smelled the freshness of spring and flowers. And tasted a sweetness he never seemed to get enough of. "Well?"

A soft longing stirred inside her. How easily she could lose herself in him, she realized. "I might need to test that again later to be sure."

Gently he kissed her once more. "Anytime."

"Are we going back to the ranch now?"

"Not yet." He smiled at a gaping Sybil. "One more place to go."

Stetson and all, he glided her around a roller rink, his arm secure at her waist.

Laughing, her eyes on her feet, she held on tightly to his arm. The last time she'd been on roller skates, she'd been eight years old. "Do people in town know you're loony?"

"They learned that long ago when the Pritchards' bull got loose, and I rode him down Main Street."

To her amazement, she stayed upright on the skates. And had fun. When had she ever given herself time for fun? It hadn't been a part of her childhood, and as an adult, she'd been working too hard to succeed. It was strange to her, but she felt different. Perhaps her aunt had been right that she'd needed to slow down, to enjoy life more.

With Denver, she carted groceries from the store to the truck. She'd come with him to be safe, true, but she also saw this as an opportunity to learn more about him. Oddly, she was learning more about herself. Scanning the town's main street, she realized how wrong she'd been before arriving in Whispering Pines. She'd had preconceived notions. A past filled with small towns where only a gas station and a few stores existed had colored her judgment of all country towns. She didn't know why that had happened, only that she felt differently now.

Standing in the doorway of the grocery store, Adele grinned. "You two come back soon," she said as if Kelly would always be around.

Kelly smiled in answer and said nothing. She'd vowed long ago not to think about tomorrows with any man. When it was time for it to end, as she knew it would, she'd feel more pain than she'd expected. But she'd also have more memories.

Kelly helped Lorna unpack groceries, then snatched up her notes to closet herself in the den. A surprise phone call stopped her. Relief swept over her at the sound of Jamie's voice.

"I couldn't believe it when Aunt Jean told me where you were."

"Where are you?" Kelly asked. "Are you okay?"

"I'm fine." With hesitation, Jamie went on. "We were in Albuquerque on Monday, El Paso on Tuesday and Tulsa on Thursday."

"And you're happy?"

"Yes." Uncertainty edged her sister's voice. "I know you didn't think I would be with him. He flirts a lot while performing, but he's good to me. And I'll tame him," she said with the light airy sureness of youth.

You shouldn't have to, Kelly wanted to say. "I can hardly wait to hear about everything when you come back to Phoenix," she said instead.

"Oh, Kelly, I was worried you'd—well, you were so against this."

"Only one thing matters."

"What?"

"I love you," Kelly told her softly.

"Oh, Kel," her sister returned on a choked sound.

What changed your mind? Jamie had asked before they'd ended the conversation.

Kelly had had no answer. Perhaps she was learning to see things more clearly.

Strolling into the den, she thought about the story she'd write. Mary Ellen Casey wouldn't be part of it. Whatever mystery of the past lingered for Denver and his father, she didn't need it revealed to write her story about him. By coming to the ranch, she'd seen the man beneath the public image.

During the past few days, she'd heard the compliments he offered to Lorna about her cooking. He'd spoken them with the ease that someone else said good morning. She'd seen him playing Frisbee with a cowboy's nine-year-old son. She'd heard him sing a soft lullaby to a cowhand's new daughter. She'd been in the presence of a man with an enormous capacity for giving, who was as rooted to the land as some of the hundred-year-old trees on the ranch.

For the next hour, she incorporated those observations and her notes into the story she'd started. Her shoulders stiff, she leaned back in the chair and emptied film out of the camera. Inserting a new roll, she doubted she'd taken any award-winning photographs, but with luck, most of them would be passable.

Stretching, she felt her stomach rumble and pushed back her chair. Recalling the leftover chocolate cake from last night's dinner, she hit the kitchen door and called out to Lorna. It was then she heard the yells.

Through the kitchen window, she viewed a scene that made fear rise in her throat. Men were hunkered down in a corral, circling someone.

Denver. It was her first thought as she flew from the house. Breathing hard, she pushed her way through the crowd. Denver, Will and Lorna were bent over Charlie. Her throat closed as she saw the gash on his head. "What happened?"

"A mustang kicked him," someone behind her volunteered over the wail of an ambulance.

Pale, Lorna rose stiffly under the command of Will's arm around her. "You go with him in the ambulance," he told her. "We'll follow in the truck."

Kelly stared at Charlie on the stretcher, at Lorna.

Dirt marring his cheek, his shirt damp with sweat, Denver issued an order to one of the ranch hands and whirled around toward his truck.

Kelly fell in step with him. "Are you going to the hospital?"

Grim, he nodded. "I don't know how long we'll be."

She stepped away as they reached the back of the truck and rushed to the passenger's side. "I'm going, too."

Chapter Eleven

Caught in traffic, they arrived to see Lorna coming down the hall from the emergency room.

"How's Charlie?" Will asked anxiously.

"They're taking X rays. We have to wait," she said faintly.

Kelly settled beside Lorna. "He'll be all right." The token reassurance seemed so shallow, but what words were right at such a moment?

Tears misting her eyes, Lorna gripped her hands tightly together. "Yes, he'll be all right," she repeated, sounding determined not to cry.

With stunning clarity, Kelly recalled Will's words of warning about the harshness surrounding them. She stared at Lorna, who was wrestling with herself to be strong. Was this what all ranch women had to learn just to survive in the country? Kelly tossed aside disturbing thoughts. Now wasn't the time for them. "How many times have you told me that he's the toughest, orneriest man alive?"

Lorna managed a slim smile. "He is that."

Closing a hand over hers, Kelly struggled to keep conversation going. She prodded Lorna to reminisce, forced her to think about the great meal she'd make her husband when he came home.

Will stood at the window, just staring out as if imprisoned, lines deepening on his face. On the other side of Lorna, Denver comforted her with the love of a son. Amazingly he stirred her smiles, made her forget, even if only for a second. But every second he eased the agony of waiting, he gave her more strength.

Time crawled. Kelly drained the coffee in her cup and stared at the clock above the emergency room doors. More people wandered into the waiting room. The inane chatter of a television talk show mingled with the hushed conversations. For what seemed the hundredth time, Kelly glanced at the clock. She was checking the accuracy of her watch when the swinging doors of the emergency room swayed open. Instead of the doctor, a waiting room receptionist strolled out.

Five more minutes passed before the doctor came through the doors.

Lorna rose rigidly, dazed eyes on him, her back ramrod straight.

"He has a concussion and a broken leg." He offered a semblance of a smile. "But he's conscious."

Audibly Lorna sighed and sagged with relief against Denver. "Thank God. Can I see him?"

"If you're Lorna, you'd better. He's in there insisting on seeing you."

Tears streaked her cheeks. "I love that old coot."

"Go," Will urged. "I'll wait for you."

She started to step away, then turned back, her eyes sweeping over all of them. "I couldn't have made it without all of you here."

"We're family," Will said gruffly. "Where the hell do you think we'd be?"

Lorna's smile widened. In passing, she tapped his cheek affectionately.

Pleased yet uncomfortable with the affection, he looked away. "I'll stay until Lorna's ready to leave," he announced.

Kelly smiled at the warmth of love she'd witnessed. They were family. Not by blood but linked by unselfish love for one another.

"Tired?"

Denver laced his fingers with hers.

For the first time in hours, she allowed fatigue to take hold and noticed a similar weariness marked his face. "No more than you are." Slipping the strap of her purse to her shoulder, she rose with him.

"We couldn't have helped her through these moments the same way you did. She needed a woman with her. A friend."

"I wish I could have helped more." Muscles tight, she rolled a shoulder. "You did pretty good, too."

He pushed open the exit door. "Guess it's time you realized something."

Preceding him out the door, she looked over her shoulder. "And what's that?"

"We're good together."

Another week passed, and Kelly became more immersed in the life around her. With Charlie convalescing, Denver was even busier. She learned about ranching, more than she expected. She knew now how they gathered cattle, vaccinated and milked, and had even helped bottle-feed calves. Ranch sounds had become familiar to her: the whistling of a lasso, the snorting of horses, the earthy words of cowhands, the evening bell courting men from the bunkhouse to file into the cookhouse for dinner.

Though she still found getting up so early almost painful, she'd begun awakening before seven, a civilized hour in her mind.

Four-thirty wasn't, she mentally grumbled as she opened her eyes to the sound of Denver moving around the room. It was dark except for the light from a small lamp on the end table. With a sigh, she eased herself from Denver's bed. Shivering beneath the predawn chill in the room, she dressed swiftly, with a reminder that she was doing him a favor.

Last night, she'd have promised him anything. When he'd asked her to get up with him the next morning, she'd said yes without a second thought.

Well, she hadn't been thinking too much about anything at that moment. Tired now, she decided that it really wasn't fair for a man to ask a woman to do something when she was swimming beneath shivers because of his caresses.

Last night when he'd drawn her into his room instead of coming to hers, she'd noticed nothing in it, her mind too filled with him. Smoothing out the comforter, she saw now the bow and arrow propped in one corner near the heavy oak desk.

Pivoting away from the closet, Denver shrugged into a shirt. "You don't have to make the bed."

"Well, I'm not going to leave it like this," she said, going on with the task.

He crossed to stand on the opposite side of the bed. He liked the way she looked when she was sleepy, her eyes hooded, her hair tousled from his hands. Bending over, he pulled up the comforter. "Okay?"

"Almost," she said, reaching for a pillow.

Amused but not surprised, he turned away. Her orderly mind never tolerated clutter. No messiness, not even in relationships, he reminded himself. The way he saw it theirs was one big mess. He'd tried to rationalize his feelings about her. Did he love her? She wasn't an easy woman to understand. Despite making love with him, she was reluctant to let her emotions take her beyond passion.

He had no problem with her ambition, her drive, her determination, even her independence. He respected all of those traits in her because the same ones had helped him succeed. But she also possessed a fair amount of mistrust and a hell of a lot of caution. Only late at night in bed did he know the generosity, the tenderness, the vulnerability she shielded.

Kelly fluffed a pillow. The room was masculine with few frills. Deep blue drapes matched the dominant color in the patchwork quilt, and a huge painting of a nighttime shoot-out by the Western artist Charles Russell adorned the wall. She smiled at the sight of the shiny championship buckle on the dresser. He wouldn't wear it here. Here, Denver Casey, world rodeo champion, became ranchman, son, friend.

Standing, she ran a smoothing hand over the comforter then stilled. On the lower shelf of the bedside table was a small photograph. Dark haired, in her early thirties, the woman was breathtakingly beautiful, with creamy skin and a smile that was familiar to Kelly.

He rarely talked about his mother, yet he'd kept a photograph of her. To cherish her memory? If he did, why did he shun talking about her?

Looking over his shoulder, Denver stilled in buckling his belt as he saw her holding the photograph. He'd forgotten it was there. He rarely looked at it. He simply kept it. He wasn't sure if it was to remind him of her or of what she'd done.

Aware of his stare, Kelly measured her words before asking. "Do you ever see her?"

He buckled his belt. "She's dead." Sensing there was no way to avoid it, he faced her squarely. "We don't mention her name around here."

Stunned by the coldness in his voice, she dropped to sit on the mattress. "Was she so bad?"

"What are you doing?" he asked, holding a palm out to her.

Because she wasn't sure how to handle the moment, she tried to make light of it. "I was curious."

"Curious." He rolled the word around as if contemplating it. "A necessary trait for your job?"

Kelly stiffened slightly. Long ago, she'd stopped thinking about him as part of her job. She couldn't explain why what he harbored inside him was so important to her, but she'd never have written about it, even if she knew. She'd never wanted to bare his soul to the public.

"Don't you know who I am by now?" she asked. She swallowed down a hard knot in her throat.

"Don't you know I care about you?" Care didn't come close to the emotion she aroused within him. He closed the distance between them and drew her to a stand. If he told her that no other woman had ever meant so much to him, that he longed for the sight of her when they were apart, that just the touch of her hand eased aching muscles, she'd run. And that scared him more than a rejection.

"I'm sorry."

Denver stroked her shoulder. Trust teetered in the shadows. "No, I'm sorry."

She watched his eyes soften. Encouraged, she stepped closer. As he drew her into his arms, she pressed her face close to his. "You had a right to be angry."

He hadn't been angry. Scared. He was scared of what she might learn, and scared if he kept his secret, he'd lose her. Scared that he'd probably lose her no matter what else happened.

Drawing back, he saw her troubled frown. This wasn't what he'd wanted to bring into her life. "Are you stalling?" he asked, forcing a smile to stir hers. "Get dressed."

Kelly drew a long breath. She wanted him to trust her, but how could she ask that of him when she was strangling their relationship with her doubts?

Reaching for a sheepskin-lined vest, he glanced back at her. He knew now he wanted her to stay. He wanted to keep her close, to know she was his. But he couldn't talk about love, not when too many uncertainties still plagued him. "Ready?"

"Yes." Kelly tugged on her boot. "Where are we going?"

"You'll see," he said, taking her hand.

Kelly always believed she was a good sport. She gave herself an extra pat on the back half an hour later.

Sitting on a boulder, she shivered and cradled her hands around the coffee cup he'd just offered her. "I can't fish," she said for the third time.

"Sure you can."

Kelly gave him a doubting look.

Smiling indulgently at her, he draped a blanket around her shoulders.

While she appreciated the warmth of the cloth, she thought again that she could have done without this experience. "Fish is your favorite food?" she asked, finding it difficult to believe any sane person would get up this early to freeze unless he had a craving for fresh trout.

"Not really." He baited a hook. "But I promised Lorna I'd catch fish for tonight's dinner."

"Why was I included?" she asked between sips of coffee, eyeing the wiggling worm. She hoped he didn't expect her to do that.

Softly he chuckled at her aggrieved tone. "To keep me company."

"I don't want to complain but—"

"I can see that," he said on a laugh.

She pulled a face at his back. "But couldn't we have done this at a more civilized hour?"

"Probably."

"Then, why didn't we?"

"You've been asking a lot of questions for so early in the morning." He paused in hooking the bait. "Usually you're the early-morning quiet type."

She huddled in the blanket he'd given her. "I'm trying to keep my teeth from chattering."

"Think about something else." Standing, he tossed the line into the water.

She watched the wind toss his dark hair. "Do you have any childhood pranks to share with me?"

"Hundreds." He let out the line slowly, then wedged the pole between two rocks.

At his silence, she gave another question a try to stop thinking about how cold she was. "Was Sue Ann

Kimball your first love?'' Her head bent, she rubbed her hands together. This was not her idea of fun.

She looked up to find him smiling, bending over her. On second thought, maybe it was, she mused.

''You are.''

It would be so easy to let herself believe in love again, to take his words to heart. She threw part of the blanket over him and stretched for a smile. ''I thought you were going to fish.''

''Later,'' he said, pressing her back to the ground.

Later was sunrise.

By the time they neared the house, a sheet of gray was moving across the prairie, the wind driving it and whipping at the windmill.

''We're in for a storm,'' he said, slanting a look up at the gathering clouds that carried the promise of rain.

Kelly nodded but was preoccupied. She sniffed hard at her hands and cast a distasteful look at the string of fish he was carrying. Today had definitely been a first. She still couldn't believe she'd actually touched one of the wiggling fish. ''My hands stink,'' she said when they entered the house.

Amusement stirred his smile. ''You have time for a bath before breakfast.''

''Want to join me?'' One foot on the stairs, she sent him a come-hither look. ''I'll get out the bubbles.''

''Bubbles?'' He stilled in reaching for her. ''I'll pass.''

Kelly kept going. "I'll make it worthwhile," she called out, showing the good grace not to giggle until he'd disappeared into the kitchen.

By eleven, Kelly had finished her work on the computer. Ambling out of the den, she planned to ride Sunbeam. She was a step from the door when Lorna called out.

"Phone for you." She handed Kelly the receiver. "He asked for Denver, but said he could talk to you."

The detective's message was brief. She and Denver needed to come back for the trial. Tonight, she mused, setting the receiver back in its cradle. She had only tonight with Denver and then—

And then, nothing. They would go their separate ways.

There was no and then.

Kelly rejoined Lorna in the kitchen.

Intent on her task for the evening's party, Lorna broke eggs into a bowl. "Guess you'll be telling Denver about the phone call."

"Yes."

"We're going to miss . . ." She paused and brushed her fingers across Kelly's cheek. "I'm going to miss having you around for a while. It's been nice to have another woman to talk to any time."

"You've been a good friend," Kelly said softly, more shaken than she'd expected.

"When you come back, I'll tell you all about some of the people you're going to meet tonight at the barbecue."

Kelly swung around, dumbfounded. *When she came back?*

"It's kind of cold for a barbecue, but folks around here know if they wait for good weather to do anything, they'll get nothing done. They'll start showing up around three this afternoon."

Kelly turned away from the window and the men hauling their saddles toward the corral as if in a hurry. "Do you know where Denver is?"

"He's out riding in the canyon. Some cattle wandered away from the others. They could get lost."

Kelly scanned a distant ridge. If cattle could get lost, couldn't a man? Feeling restless and uneasy suddenly, she volunteered to go to the root cellar for jars of applesauce.

Dampness, the dirt floor, the rows of jars filled with carrots, beets, potatoes and winter squash revived a memory. One year, her family had stayed long enough in a little town near Midland, Texas, for her mother to grow a skimpy vegetable garden. She'd canned that year, taking advantage of the root cellar. And ended up leaving most of her work behind when Ray had come home one afternoon, telling her he'd been laid off. It was time to leave. Always it had been time to leave.

Kelly stepped out of the root cellar and took the jars to Lorna. Nerves on edge, she hurried to the stable. She needed to be alone. Quickly she saddled Sunbeam. Something edging sorrow knotted her throat as she realized this was the last time she'd ride the horse. Nearby, a crow cawed. She squinted against the sun exploding from behind dark clouds. At the top of cliffs alive with orange and salmon-colored streaks, a vulture circled. This wasn't her life, she tried to remember. It never could be. She had her job, her life back in the city.

She squinted at the distant land, hoping to see Denver riding in. Was that what all ranch women felt at the end of the day? Did they worry when their men rode out into the canyons?

Oh, God, how had she come to this? How often had she seen her mother staring out a window, waiting for Ray to come home because she'd allowed her life, her thoughts, to revolve around one man?

Frowning, she swung around, drawn to the distant thundering sound of horses hooves. She stared at the high ridge beyond the ranch buildings. Riders appeared. Raising her hand, she shaded her eyes from the glare of the sun and searched until she spotted Denver. And she knew. In that one instant, she knew. She loved him.

Within an hour, cars and trucks began arriving. Bearing pots and covered plates, women filed into the kitchen. The smoke and smells of a tangy barbecue sauce wafted on the air. People gathered near the long tables, greeting one another warmly. Teenagers huddled on nearby bales of hay, trying to ignore the raucous shouts of younger children playing tag or throwing Frisbees.

Denver had told her that he'd never lost his yearning for the ranch during all the years rodeoing. She

understood why now. He had a place he called home.
The land was his legacy, the people as close as family.

She enjoyed the camaraderie, felt comfortable with
strangers in a world far from the one she'd known
most of her life. But despite the good humor around
her, she also felt apprehensive. Too many people were
assuming as one woman put it, that she was "Denver's lady." Talk about other women's weddings made
her stomach flutter.

Throughout the evening, she heard similar comments. With a wink or a coy smile, people implied or
alluded to some commitment between her and Denver. For all of the open space around her, Kelly was
beginning to feel trapped as much as by her own emotions as the assumptions of others.

"Why the frown?" Denver caught her by the waist
and hugged her against him.

Kelly shunned her own troubled thoughts. "We got
a phone call," she said as an excuse. "We have to go
back tomorrow."

So the moment had come. Since they'd arrived, he'd
avoided thinking about when they would go back. It
had been too easy to drift under some fantasy cloud
and pretend.

As neighbors began to leave, the chill of evening
descended on them. Leaning against the porch banis-
ter, Kelly listened to the howl of a coyote. Denver's
laugh mingled with it as he strolled with a neighbor to
look at the ebony colt he'd been taming.

Kelly dropped to a porch step, listening to distant
thunder. More than once, panic had seized her as she

acknowledged how easy it would be to accept everything around her. She couldn't say she'd been unhappy. Just the opposite. Being with Denver, enjoying the freedom to ride Sunbeam every day, yet able to work on the computer, she hadn't been bored. But could she accept his world?

The sound of rain pounding on the roof pulled her from her thoughts. A crack of lightning jolted her to a stand.

Inside the house, lights flickered. With a rush of movement, the door flew open and Will strolled down the steps and past her, muttering something about checking on the horses.

Kelly glanced again at the threatening sky, then wandered into the kitchen to help Lorna.

She'd already lit an old-time oil lamp and was adding detergent to the hot water for the dinner dishes. "Denver will have the generator working in a few minutes."

A dish towel in her hand, Kelly joined Lorna at the sink.

"You're kind of quiet," Lorna observed.

Kelly couldn't say why, but all day feelings had been churning inside her that she couldn't explain. Aware of Lorna's stare, she mustered a smile. "I'm waiting for you to tell me one of your stories."

Lorna slanted a feigned, narrow-eyed look at her. "Are you telling me I'm a blabbermouth?"

"A delightful one," Kelly said lightly.

"Well, that's okay then."

Kelly grabbed a handful of silverware. "Do you miss your own place?"

"Not anymore. We're getting older. A ranch is a lot of work." She plunged a hand into the sudsy water. "We miss not having young'uns. But Denver's sort of like one of our own." She smiled, then laughed in private amusement. "I remember one day when we still owned our own place. Denver was about ten then. Charlie came here to deliver a stud for service. Denver was in the corral with a mustang. Charlie came home and told me that Denver had pulled rank on one of the cowhands who tried to stop him from riding the horse. Ten years old and acting bossy." Lorna cackled. "Sure, if he didn't ride that horse. And then broke his arm when he got bucked off. Charlie and I drove him into the doctor's."

Kelly picked up a dish from the rack. "Where was Will?"

"Not around." Lorna wiped the back of her hand across her cheek. "If he had been, he would have stopped him." She winked at Kelly. "Though I think Will kind of liked his gumption."

Kelly couldn't keep herself from asking. "What about his mother?"

She wagged her head. "We don't talk about her."

"I don't understand that," Kelly said, confused.

"There's nothing to understand. She never paid attention to what was going on. Always too busy doing her nails, or something."

Lorna turned on the spigot and rinsed a sudsy dish under the water. The sound of water rushing over the soapy plate filled the room. "They just don't talk about her," Lorna said softly. "Will paid for her funeral because she had no one. That's the last time I heard either of them mention her name."

Kelly didn't understand. Other women left and divorced their husbands. Other children groped their way through the misery of a divorce without cutting all ties with a parent. What else had happened?

With the bang of the door behind them, Kelly looked back. Soaked, his hair plastered against his scalp, Denver gave a quick shudder. "Damn." He tugged off his boots and set them by the door.

"I taught him that," Lorna said, grinning with maternal pride.

Kelly laughed as he rolled his eyes heavenward in response to her words.

"What other secrets have you been telling her?" he asked with good humor.

Lorna's lips curled slightly. "We're just doing some lady talk here."

"That's called gossip, isn't it?"

"You always were a big smart aleck."

"Quit telling her all my good points." He stepped forward and touched the curve of Kelly's hip. "Don't pay any attention to her."

As he sauntered out of the kitchen, Lorna grinned at her. "He has a lot of good in him."

Kelly picked up another dish. "I know."

Finished with the dishes, she wandered upstairs to her room. She stripped and slipped on her oversize football jersey, then snatched up her robe. She was lonely for him, she realized. All day, she'd been lonely for him, wishing they were alone as she'd shared him with other people. She took a deep breath, then swung around in response to the door opening behind her. Love. She didn't want to feel it for him and knew she had no choice.

"Hi," he said, smiling in that slow way of his that had weakened her to him from the start. "I thought you might like company."

When the door clicked behind him, she answered the need inside her and rushed to him. "You thought right," she said, an impatience that was new swarming in on her.

"You know what?" Lightly he ran a hand down her back and pushed her against him. "I wanted you in the kitchen."

She lifted her chin to let his mouth explore her throat. "In the kitchen?"

He heard the smile in her voice but he was serious. Deadly serious. "I want you all the time," he whispered, bringing her against him. "Sounds crazy, doesn't it?"

Her lashes fluttered as he spread feather-light kisses from her throat to her collarbone. "Not to me."

"I always want more," he murmured, nibbling at her collarbone.

She closed her eyes. As if it was the first time, she sought his mouth with a hungry kiss, running a hand over his head, savoring the thick coarse texture of his hair beneath her fingers.

Though she would have rushed, he moved slowly. In the darkness of the bedroom, he knelt with her on the bed and drew off her jersey. Whispering kisses quickly became deeper.

He dragged her even closer. Mouths clinging, they fell back on the bed. She answered the tongue plunging into her mouth, matched the hands demanding more, though his movements were slow and stirring. She felt a heat beginning to warm his flesh that matched the fire bubbling within her.

As his mouth searched hers, thoughts tumbled from her mind. Only feelings dominated her. Naked, she felt cherished as every caress, every moist stroke of his tongue across her breasts and down her belly carried one message. His lovemaking was a gift of tenderness. He drew back once, his eyes dark and hooded with desire. Then, again, he touched with a gentleness, with the sensuous slowness of a lover who treasured her. Unlike before when he'd made her want, now he made her ache.

She arched against him as he drew a nipple into his mouth again. Slowly, leisurely, he stroked and caressed, and desperation began to float over her. More than desire led them then. Flesh against flesh. Pleasure for pleasure. Stroke for stroke. They tasted and touched. She couldn't think, could barely breathe. Gasping softly, she pressed him closer to her as his mouth coaxed and seduced. She had to give, to please. To love him.

Night enveloped them. Outside, the wind howled. Thunder rumbled. A different kind of storm raged between them. She clutched him to her and abandoned everything she'd ever been certain about to him—to this moment.

Denver scrambled for control, but it was the beginning of the end. As she tore the breath from him, the choice no longer belonged to him. He rolled her with him, and through a veil of passion, he heard her murmured words.

"I need you."

Need. Did she realize she'd said that to him? With his hands on her hips, he urged her to him. Each time they'd loved, he'd felt her giving more. She wouldn't like knowing that. She'd want to believe they were still two separate people with two different lives. They weren't anymore. More than passion, more than trembling pleasure brought them together. Love, fierce and sharp, mingled with passion. Feelings unlike he'd ever had before made him race. Quickly, almost desperately, he lowered himself to her. This was more than the blending of flesh, he thought, while he could still think. As her legs wrapped around him, love bound their souls. She loved him. She might never admit it. But he believed she loved him.

His face inches from hers, he searched her eyes. Slowly he moved until the need possessing him was hers, too. Then nothing mattered but the heat. He whispered her name as the fire engulfed them. Her arms gripped his back, her body arched against him, and they rose against the blaze together. She was his. At this moment, she was his.

Chapter Twelve

Kelly knew she'd slept, but she opened her eyes to shadows. The luminous dial on her wristwatch read one-thirty. Wide-awake, she couldn't believe so little time had passed.

Taking care not to awaken Denver, she slid out from under the covers. While she shrugged on her robe, she crossed to the window. The night sky exploded with lightning, jagged fingers dancing to the earth. Thunder rumbled as if threatening to shake the walls.

Sighing, she wandered out of the room and down the stairs. If she couldn't sleep anyway, then what harm could a cup of coffee do?

She started for the kitchen but saw the front door open and detoured toward it, instead. On the porch, puffing his pipe, Will merely glanced at her. Kelly stalled at the door, uncertain if she should join him. In all the time she'd been there, she'd never felt he was comfortable around her.

"Too much noise for you?" he asked.

Encouraged, she opened the screen door and stepped outside. "It's quite a spectacle."

"A person sees everything more clearly out here." He continued to stare at the night sky brightening with streaks of light. "Have you enjoyed being here?"

Uncertain, Kelly moved closer to the edge of the porch near him. "Yes," she answered, a hand on the skirt of her robe as the wind whipped it around her legs.

"I didn't think Denver would ever let any woman get so close."

His words should have pleased her, but she saw no friendliness in his eyes.

"He's in his thirties, past the age around here for settling down." His shoulders moved with a silent laugh. "But then there's Dooley who's pushing forty and thinking about it." He raised his head, his eyes suddenly challenging hers. "My son thinks you love him. I don't. If you did love him, you wouldn't be snooping."

Kelly reared back, aware, almost painfully in that second, that there was nothing friendly about his feelings for her. "I've only asked questions to learn about Denver," she said as a defense.

"Or to dig up something on him?"

"No." She pushed hair blown by the wind back from her eyes. "I care too much about him to hurt him."

"You want to know about his mother, don't you?"

The chill of the rainy wind cut through her robe. She'd thought Will's opinion of her shouldn't matter. But it did. He was Denver's father, his closest friend, his partner. "I want to understand," she said, trying to explain. "She's gone, but she haunts him and this ranch. When I've needed him, he's been there for me," she said to explain. "I'd like to do the same for him, but he won't tell me."

"She meant nothing to him."

Incredulous, Kelly shook her head. How could he believe that? "The photograph of her in Denver's room says differently."

Will's head jerked in her direction. Even under the mantle of darkness, she could see that he'd paled. "He doesn't have a photograph."

"Yes, he does." She saw confusion sweep across his face and instantly wished she'd never mentioned the photograph. "It's natural for him to have it, to hold on to some part of her," she said to ease his mind.

Anger tightened his features. "No, it isn't. She was no good. A beautiful woman with a heart of stone." Beneath the shadowed light, his eyes looked like crystal. "You say you care about him. We'll see. *I'll* tell you about her."

Kelly drew back. "No." She didn't want to hear this from him. Unless Denver told her, she didn't want to know the haunting secret these two men shared.

He gazed out at the night sky alive with an electrifying show. "She didn't leave," he went on as if not hearing her. "I ran her off the ranch."

At first, Kelly was certain she'd misunderstood, but she saw the pain of a prideful man visible in his eyes.

"She was having an affair."

In that moment, she knew he was testing her, giving her the truth to see what she'd do with it.

He shifted his shoulders. "Denver came home from school and caught her in bed with the man."

"Oh, God," she whispered, her stomach squeezing as she thought of the boy who'd witnessed that moment.

"I threw her out." As if pained, Will rubbed a hand over the back of his neck and released a labored breath. "She never belonged here, but she wanted to stay because of her son. I wouldn't let her."

Nothing was ever so simple. Her heart aching for both the son and the father, she started to reach out to Will, then stopped herself. Blame it on her tendency to analyze everything, but Kelly couldn't—no, she didn't—accept his words so simply. Denver had rejected her. Why would an unfaithful wife whose son had witnessed her infidelity want to stay? The set of Will's shoulders, the firmness of his jaw declared a man who wouldn't forgive or forget easily. "She didn't want to stay, did she?"

Instead of answering, he averted his gaze. The gesture was more telling than he knew. She almost cursed her ability to ferret out information. Sometimes, it came too easily.

"What's going on?"

She spun around to find Denver in the doorway. His hair tousled, he wore only his jeans despite the chill in the air.

Filled with anger at himself, Will lashed out at him. "You shouldn't have brought her here."

Denver turned a questioning look on her.

Her breath quickening, she rushed out her words before she lost all chance to defend herself. "I didn't ask. It happened. It just happened." She glanced from him to Will. "Nothing I've heard is anyone's business but yours and Denver's. I don't write for the tabloids. I promise you won't see it in print."

Will gave a shake of his head as if prodding Denver. "You going to believe her?"

Blocked out were the roar of the wind and rumble of thunder. The quietness stretched between them and pounded in her ears. Straining for a breath, she moved quickly toward the door, shaken by the distrust that clung to the air. *I'm telling the truth,* she wanted to scream.

"Can you trust her not to tell?" she heard Will ask.

Would her name, too, become one never mentioned? She kept walking. She'd seen so much anguish in the eyes of both men. And so much loathing. Years had passed; they hadn't forgotten or forgiven one woman.

She rushed up the stairs to her room. Nothing she said would make a difference. Denver had to believe in her, trust her. If he didn't, then everything they'd shared meant nothing. She crawled into bed and lay still, staring into the darkness, remembering more than Will's words. The torment in his eyes haunted her. All these years had passed, yet he still revealed fury. And something else. In his eyes, she'd seen shame and sorrow. He'd been broken by one woman.

She closed her eyes to block out her thoughts, but when the door opened, she jerked around. "Denver."

"He's worried," he said softly. Shadows shrouded him as he tugged off his boots and yanked down his jeans. In the stillness of the room, his breaths, slow and steady, revealed nothing.

She shifted to see his face. She knew now he'd kept his life private for one reason—to protect a proud man from reliving the shame of having had an unfaithful wife. "You know better." Never before had she wanted so badly to wrap her arms around someone and comfort him. "Don't you?"

"I wouldn't be here if I didn't," he said in a voice huskier than usual, as he slid under the covers beside her.

She took care with her words. "Is he angry at me?"

"No," he said so softly she barely heard him.

She inched closer but didn't touch him. "I meant what I said."

With unblinking eyes, he stared at the dark ceiling. "I know."

Kelly slid her hand across his chest. Cold. He felt so cold.

"He didn't tell you everything." Beneath the hand resting on his chest, she felt him draw a long breath as if cleansing his lungs. "The man was one of the cow-hands."

"Don't. You don't have to tell me," she whispered.

But he did. For over twenty years, that day had been locked behind silence. Instead of healing, the sores had festered. "Yeah, I do," he murmured. "There were others. He wasn't the only one. We learned that later." Weariness crept into his voice as if he were lifting a burden he'd carried too long. "When I walked in, she—she yelled that I shouldn't tell him. I thought she loved him and didn't want her marriage destroyed." A mirthless tone edged his voice. "But she really didn't give a damn. She wanted to leave but not without money. She knew he wouldn't give her a dime if he learned she was with another man."

She touched his cheek, wishing for some magic to ease his pain.

Lightning illuminated his face in an eerie glow. "Will walked in only minutes after me as the cow-hand was rushing out. He knew what had been going on. I don't think I've ever seen him so angry. She screamed that she'd never loved him. She'd only married him for the money. She hadn't expected to live out in some damn wilderness. She hated her life and his damn ranch."

Denver reached a hand back and gripped a rail of the brass headboard. Memories seemed like yesterday now. The harsh words, the feeling of helplessness, and later, the sight of tears in his father's eyes. "I went to her. I didn't understand. She kept packing, throwing clothes into a suitcase. She was angry." He felt pressure building in his chest, a hard, heavy pressure that was threatening to close off his windpipe. "She yelled at me. Hadn't I heard what she'd said to him?" His voice softened. "I'd heard. But I couldn't believe she'd never loved him. She tossed clothes into a suitcase, ranting that coming to the ranch had been a mistake, her marriage had been a mistake."

Too clearly Kelly was seeing what a twelve-year-old boy had witnessed. As he made a soft sound as if straining to breathe, she closed her eyes, her throat beginning to burn.

He shook his head, wishing he could get the images of that night out of his mind. They'd never leave, he knew. They were images meant to linger because of words too painful to ever be forgotten. "She grabbed her suitcase, then stopped at the door and looked at me. She was angry at me, too. She yelled that I should stop looking at her like it was all her fault. None of it had been. It had all been a mistake. I'd been a mistake. She wouldn't have been there if she'd never gotten pregnant."

Pain clenched in Kelly's chest. She felt almost dizzy from it. She couldn't speak as his agony invaded her as if it were her own.

He turned flat, emotionless eyes on her, eyes filled with unspeakable torment. "I thought I'd misunderstood her. I hadn't. She yelled it again. She said she'd never wanted to get pregnant and lose her figure. She'd never wanted even one bawling brat around her."

He paused for a second, not believing the same sick feeling was clutching his stomach. He'd had it that day, but he was a man now, not a boy. "Later," he said more firmly, "when she was ready to go out the door, she yelled at Will, told him he could have me."

Kelly raised her head from his chest.

Unseeing eyes looked past her, through her. "She stared at him, not me. I don't know, maybe she didn't realize I was still near. She smiled at him. But it wasn't really a smile. Told him it would serve him right to be stuck forever with someone else's son."

"Someone else's . . ." *Someone else's.* Stunned, she struggled to breathe evenly as his words sunk in.

"That's when I learned Will wasn't my father," he added in a stronger but flat-sounding tone. "I walked out of the room and never saw her again."

For a moment, she couldn't think. Tears for him smarted her eyes. She tried to focus and couldn't. In the darkness, she sought his hand. It seemed like such an empty gesture.

"Will had known. I hadn't." Shifting, he drew her tighter against him, needing her warmth. "He never treated me differently."

"And your father?" she managed to ask.

"Will Casey is my father." He swallowed hard against the ache constricting his throat. "In his mind, in mine, I am his son."

Furiously she blinked back tears and drew back to look at him. "I'm sorry." Sorry for delving too deeply, for learning a secret he'd meant never to reveal.

He touched her head, urging it back to his chest. He wanted to forget. Forget everything for a while. He listened to her soft breathing and closed his eyes to ban everything. Mostly he wanted to forget that she'd leave, too.

The pounding of rain against the roof lulled him. It seemed strange, but he felt no more tightness in his chest. Peace. He recognized it instantly because it had eluded him for so long. At some moment, it had washed over him just as emotions for her had flooded him.

He tightened his hold on her and closed his eyes. He wanted more nights like this with her beside him. More mornings of her face being the first he'd see. Before this, he'd thought he loved her. But without trust, he'd have never told her what she deserved to know. Without her, he'd have never learned to trust.

Breathing easy, he began to drift with images of this woman, smiling, laughing, her eyes only for him. He held her against him, feeling her slow, steady breaths and knew he'd sleep now.

He did, but not for long. It wasn't haunting images of the past, but a crack, deafening in the darkness that woke him with a start. Fighting to orient himself, he glanced toward the window and the night sky.

Kelly stirred. "What's wrong?"

Rain pounded, the wind howling. Like the tail of a comet, lightning streaked downward. Denver's heart quickened. Bolting from the bed, he rushed to the window.

Drowsy, Kelly searched the dark room. He stood at the window, shoving up the window sash. Sitting up, she thought she smelled smoke. "Denver?"

"Fire," he yelled, already grabbing for his Levi's.

Before the door closed behind him, she bounded from the bed. Every person would be needed, even her. Her heart quickening, she dressed in haste, then dashed down the steps, grabbing a rain slicker off a hook near the front door. She'd seen a fire once in a small Texas hamlet near the oil fields. By the time the fire engines had arrived, an inferno had ravaged everything.

Chaos surrounded her. All around her, men, forming a sea of yellow slickers, sprinted with water buckets dangling from their hands.

From the shelter of the front porch, she peered into the darkness. A hue of red warmed the night sky. She hit the bottom step. Fat raindrops plopped on her, whipped westwardly by the wind. Beneath the lightning's illumination, she saw Denver racing for the stable adjacent to the barn, for the horses. Fierce orangish red flames danced on the roof of the barn. Smoke belched from it, then mushroomed.

Kelly tore toward the stable. Rain plummeted onto the dirt. Slippery now, it, too, played as much an enemy as the fire. Slipping twice, she nearly plowed into another hazy figure.

Will blinked against the rain. "Go inside."

"What can I do?" she yelled.

His hesitation lasted only a second. Nothing mattered but the fire. He told her to order the men to water down the stable wall closest to the barn.

She whirled around and sloshed through a puddle, mud splattering up at her. Over the wail of the wind and the pounding of rain, she shouted Will's order at one of the men in the long lines passing buckets.

The fire teased the roof of the stables. Pushed by the wind, the smoke rolled over the roof like a giant gray cloud. The sound of the howling wind, of the rumbling thunder, of the roar and crackling of fire pounded in her ears. Her heart drumming frantically, she started running then. Running toward the stable.

She was steps from the doors and the cloud of smoke engulfing them when a firm hand gripped her arm, jolting her back. "Where the hell are you going?"

"Denver—Denver's in there." She jerked to break free, but the hand only tightened on her arm. Annoyed, frustrated, she swung around to lash out.

Will held firm. "He'll be out. Just stay here. He'll be out."

How could he be so sure? What if he didn't get out? She turned pleading eyes up at Will. "We have to do something. We have to."

He drew her against him, clutching her shoulder. "You just stay." His eyes fixed on the hazy view. "See," he said, sounding more certain as horses galloped from the opened stable doors. "He'll be out soon."

Wait. All she could do was wait. She'd spent a night with her mother waiting, then again she'd waited with Jamie in her arms after Ray was killed. It wasn't until she waited for Kevin to return that she realized how much waiting she'd done in her life. And each time, she'd lost someone she'd loved.

"Easy," Will soothed, making her aware she was trembling.

She sidled closer to him. Just as the land did, the fire challenged and fed on weakness. The heat of it fanned their faces, the smoke seeped closer. Fear slithered over her. She fought it as the rain kept pounding. It was their only real hope to control the blaze.

She squinted, blinking eyes smarting from the rain and smoke.

"Told you." Will's fingers squeezed her shoulder. "He's out."

Denver darted from a fog of smoke, leading the colt through the haze. Bedlam greeted him. His eyes burning, he bent over and gripped his knees. His first breath of fresh air hurt but he kept filling his lungs. He swallowed down an urge to vomit as he felt the clamp of a hand on his shoulder.

"Son."

"'kay. I'm okay." Denver waved him away and glanced back at the burning barn. Smoke funneled in the air. Fiery fingers licked at the roof, the roar of the blaze deafening as it dueted with the thundering rain. Another bolt of lightning split the sky miles away. With no time to spare, Denver ran toward the relay lines and took his place.

Only then did Kelly draw her first steady breath. Only then did she see the trucks of neighbors parked in helter-skelter fashion. No family could have been more supportive than the ranch hands and neighbors working even more feverishly now to battle the fire.

For minutes, they passed the buckets brimming with water. Their efforts seemed so futile. But no one stopped.

In the distance, she heard the sound of a siren resounding on the night air like the wail of a haunting apparition. It seemed like an eternity before the fire truck barreled down the dirt road.

The men fell out of line to help with the hoses. Huddling in her slicker, Kelly watched from a position near Will as the hoses were snaked across the muddy ground and water blasted at the flames.

"We're lucky, " he said. "The rain slowed the fire down."

Lucky? Her gaze sought Denver. His face darkened from the smoke, he was grinning at something one of the ranch hands had said. He had an unshakable resiliency. A fighting spirit. She smiled up at Will as she heard the shriek of another siren. "Yes," she said softly.

One wall and a portion of the roof remained standing by the time they extinguished the fire. No one had been hurt, and they'd lost no livestock. Denver strolled toward his father, only then noticing the smaller figure in a yellow slicker standing beside him. He hadn't had time to think about Kelly before this, but he'd assumed she was in the house.

Will gripped Denver's shoulder. "Could have been worse. You're really okay?"

"I'm a Casey," he said with added meaning. "Strong stock." He wiped a hand across his face, then noticed the soot streaking Kelly's. "What have you been doing?" he asked with a soft laugh.

"A damn good job of helping us," Will piped in. "She was beside me passing buckets and worrying with me about you barbecuing your backside."

Denver laughed, but in his father's eyes, he saw an acceptance of the woman standing between them.

"Boy's got no sense," Will said to Kelly, giving her arm a gentle squeeze before moving away.

She drew a shaky breath, touched by the affection Will had offered her. With it, she knew he'd offered something even more valuable—trust.

"He's wrong." Denver bent his head and kissed her lightly. "I found you."

Too many emotions had swept through her since she'd seen him dashing into the smoke and flames. Shuddering now with relief, she ran her hands over his back, then fiercely gripped him to her. With the heat of him against her, she closed her eyes against the tears that threatened to fall.

In defense, she stared at the destruction nearby and was reminded of what she'd always known. The country was harsh. It challenged and battled. And no matter what a person did, within minutes, it could steal everything away.

* * *

The rain that had begun the night before weakened to a drizzle by morning. While Denver helped clear away debris from last night's fire, Kelly typed up a final draft of her story about him. She took out the disk, pleased with the results and turned off the computer.

"You all done?"

Kelly turned toward Will. "Is Denver ready to leave?"

"He's with Homer Newman," Will said as he stepped into the den.

Recalling the guests from last night, Kelly guessed, "A thin man?"

"That's him. As yakkity as his wife." He gave her a quick smile. "There's something I want to say to you."

Kelly tensed at the seriousness that had entered his voice. "If it's about the story—"

He held up a halting hand. "Let me talk." For a moment, he did nothing but draw a deep breath as if working up the courage to speak. "I haven't put out the welcome mat for you, have I?" He jammed a hand into his jacket pocket. "Sometimes old men aren't wiser. They're just old fools. I was wrong about you."

Those words gruffly said to her meant so much more than she'd expected. She felt a tug at her heart. "Thank you."

"Seems my son grew up to be a man with a lot of sense. He was smart enough to go after you."

Did he, too, like Lorna, think she'd be back?

"It's not that I didn't like you," Will said. "But I—"

"I know. You didn't want him to be hurt."

"That's right. But don't be so easy on me." He gave her a crooked smile. "I wasn't fair to you."

Kelly realized it was the first genuine one he'd offered since she'd been there.

"I don't know why I told you what we haven't talked about in twenty years except..." A line furrowed his forehead. "I guess like my son said, you're special."

"It's good that he's had you all these years," Kelly said softly.

His smile widened. Before a breath could be drawn, Kelly found herself enveloped in a bear hug. "And now, he's got you, too."

At the doorway, Denver waited a moment until Will stepped back from her. "I thought Homer would never go home," he said, laughing.

"Told you." Will grinned at her. "He's as gabby as his wife." He turned away, chuckling at his own words.

"We should be leaving soon." They weren't words that came out easily for Denver.

Kelly nodded and picked up papers from the desk. Tension. Though she'd felt none of it during the past weeks, it and confusion were tugging at her suddenly. "I need to finish packing."

Drawing her back against him, Denver grazed her hip with his fingertips. "Want help?"

She clung to the smile she heard in his voice, not wanting to spoil her last moments with him at the ranch. Slanting a dubious look over her shoulder at him, she saw the devilment sparkling in his eyes. "You're going to help?"

"Sure." He drew the word out and grinned, his fingers playing with a button on her blouse. "You want to pack this, don't you?"

Kelly smiled slowly. "Do we have enough time for this?"

"We'll make time."

Chapter Thirteen

By two that afternoon, they were back in the city. All of Kelly's earlier tension drifted away the moment she entered her apartment with Denver. With everything familiar around her, she began to relax. She was where she belonged. It was a thought she repeated during the drive to the courthouse.

A throng of reporters and photographers were waiting for them. Jostled against her, Denver grumbled as he steered her past the crowd. "Damn."

Kelly wondered if he realized what he was giving up by dropping out of the limelight. "You didn't expect to escape this, did you?"

"I'd hoped to." He blinked as a flash blinded him, and brushed away a microphone shoved in his face.

Elbowing his way through the crowd for them, he opened the courtroom door and ignored the questions being hurled at him.

Disturbingly Kelly thought of all the times she'd done something similar to a celebrity.

Denver nudged her forward, almost protectively.

"We're a hungry group," she said with a look back at him.

She was taking it all in stride while he was hating it. He wasn't back in the city an hour, and he wished he were already driving back to the ranch. Two hours tops and he'd be back, he reminded himself for encouragement. Another thought slipped through. Two hours and she'd be gone from his life.

Nerves accompanied Kelly while she testified. The brothers decked out in blue suits aimed sullen looks at her that were meant to intimidate. Deliberately she fixed a stare on Denver. Stepping off the witness stand, she acknowledged that through the past weeks she'd looked to him often during stressful times.

As she listened to him give his brief account of that day in the convenience store, it seemed like another time to her now. So much had changed for her. Yet, nothing had, she realized. She was back where she belonged; he wasn't.

Having gathered his courage, the store's cashier offered his eyewitness testimony against the brothers. The case cemented against them, Denver urged Kelly out the door with him. They were greeted again by the media. Dodging reporters, he steered her toward her car and waited for her to pull away before he jumped into his truck.

Leaning back against her car, Kelly waited for him in the parking lot adjacent to her apartment complex. "Did you give them the slip?"

He chuckled. "It's easy to dodge nosy reporters."

She made a face. "I don't think that was a compliment." As he stepped close, she linked her hand with his. "Want some coffee?"

He wanted more time. Damn, he felt desperate for it. "You bought some?"

In retaliation to his tease, she deliberately bumped him with her hip as they passed through the doorway together. "I always had coffee." Smiling, she pressed the elevator button, then whirled around and leaned back against the wall. "I might even make you a big breakfast." Coiling her arms around his neck, she drew him closer. "If you stayed the night."

A need to bury himself in her tempted him to say yes. In his whole life, he'd never dodged difficult moments. He couldn't now, either. To stay would only postpone what seemed like the inevitable. He dragged her closer, needing the contact. He couldn't let go so easily. Because of her, he'd learned to trust. Because of her, he'd learned to believe in love. No, he thought determinedly, he damn well wasn't ready to say goodbye. He lifted his hand to her cheek. "Why don't you come back with me?"

Her stomach fluttered. One second. Two. Maybe, more passed. "I couldn't do that," she said softly, still not believing he'd asked. "We both knew I'd only be there until the trial."

He drew back more to see her face. "I changed my mind."

"Denver, I can't go back with you. Everything I have is here."

"Everything?" Frustration stirred to mingle with the start of something painful. "I love you." He grabbed her shoulders to keep her from turning away. "Does that count?"

Kelly swayed. There it was. Love. He was offering her the most valued gift in the world. Words any other woman would yearn to hear, and she wanted to run, afraid of what love could do to her. "I—you know I care about you."

Muscles in his back tightened as if preparing for a hard blow. "Just *care?*"

She averted her eyes to avoid the hurt in his. "None of this is simple."

He stretched to stay calm. "Tell me you don't love me," he demanded.

She heard the elevator doors hum open behind her. "I can't. I do love you," she admitted softly.

Intense blue eyes pinned her. "If you love me, then what the hell else matters?" He hadn't planned to say that, knew it sounded like a demand to her, but he was fumbling now, feeling the edge of his own insecurities.

She saw anger in his eyes. She realized it was the first time she'd seen him angry. And she saw hurt. "You knew how I felt. I don't like country living."

"You're fooling yourself," he flared. He wanted to reason with her and couldn't. The hurt tightened like a hard ball in his gut, the need to beg almost slipping over him.

"No, I'm not." She took a hard breath. "I have a life of my own. Here."

"You could have one with me." He wanted to shake her, to drag her against him, to make her admit and accept the love waiting for them. "I love you. I love you for your strength, for your intelligence, for your independence."

She knew love wasn't enough. Long ago, she'd learned that lesson. She'd watched its destructiveness with her mother. She'd given it before to Kevin. He'd taught her it couldn't be counted on. The only thing she could count on was herself. Because anger helped, she chose its path. "I can't give you what you want. I'm sorry. I'm really sorry."

He saw tears in her eyes and started to draw her close.

She broke free and backed up into the elevator. "Don't. Nothing will change," she said, fighting herself as much as him. "I belong here."

"You don't belong anywhere but with me." He stood for a moment, simply staring at the closing doors then swung away to keep himself from going after her. Nothing made sense to him. He'd found the woman he wanted to spend his life with. Why couldn't she want what he wanted? Why couldn't love be enough?

He yanked open the door of his truck but gave another look over his shoulder toward her apartment. He didn't belong in the city. If he could change, he would. He and Kelly knew that he'd never fit in. But she could live at the ranch. During the time she'd been with him, he'd almost forgotten that she didn't belong there.

Swearing, he ran a hand across tired eyes, hating the feeling of helplessness shadowing him. She talked about not giving up what she had. Then how the hell could she give up what they could have together?

Morning sunlight blasted against her car window, almost mocking her as she drove toward the office. Three days, she mused. Had it been three days since she'd seen him? Why did it feel like three years? Why, if she was supposed to forget him, was she feeling like this?

She'd done the right thing, she reassured herself. They both had definite ideas about what they wanted out of life, and those ideas were at opposite poles. He was offering her a life that she'd tried to forget. Here, she'd have everything she wanted.

She opened the door to her office and stared at the deflated balloons scattered around the carpet. Setting down her purse, she bent down and began picking them up. Oh, God, this wasn't easy. She could sweep them away, but the ache inside her wouldn't ease up. She'd expected regrets. What she'd never been prepared for was this awful hurt that made her want to curl up somewhere.

Sitting down at her desk, she fingered the hand-written wedding invitation that Dooley had sent her yesterday. Warmth behind her eyes warned her of tears. She wouldn't go, of course, but emotion tore at her. She'd been a part of something warm and giving for a little while. And with a kind note, one man was urging her back to it.

"I'm playing delivery boy today."

Kelly swung her chair away from the computer to see her aunt carrying a tray.

"I brought you a doughnut and coffee." She placed the tray on Kelly's desk and pulled a leather chair closer. Earlier, she'd offered sympathetic words about Kelly's melancholy over Denver.

Eyeing the chocolate doughnut her aunt set before her, Kelly frowned. The woman seated near who'd always shoved multigrain muffins at her had purchased junk food. What had changed her health-conscious aunt that she'd succumb to such an indulgence? "Is this a business meeting or brunch?"

"Both. I was craving chocolate this morning. Knowing you always do, I decided to share one of these with you. I also wanted to tell you that the article about Denver was excellent." She spooned sugar into her coffee. "It showed the private side of him, the ranchman that his employees respect, the down-home boy who never forgot his roots and friends."

Kelly nodded, pleased. What she hadn't written about was the painful memory that had haunted father and son. "I'm glad you liked it." Kelly sipped her coffee and waited. Over the rim of her coffee cup, her aunt smiled. It wasn't an ordinary smile. She looked ebullient.

"I also came to tell you that I've been seeing—someone."

"Someone?" Her aunt was a staunch career woman. How was it possible that she'd allowed a man to enter her life?

"An old classmate. He's a widower and well, we went out to dinner and then to the theater and then..." She paused, seeming alert to her girlish rambling. "I've been seeing a great deal of him." She set her coffee cup on Kelly's desk. "Years ago, I'd walked away from this man to pursue my career."

Kelly dropped the doughnut in her hand. "Were you in love with him?"

Her aunt's smile softened to almost a wistful one. "He was my first love, Kelly," she said as if that explained everything.

Kelly tried to take everything in quickly. "If you loved him, then why didn't you marry him?"

"Oh, I don't know." She looked so puzzled by her own words. "Your grandparents wanted me to go to Europe with them, and his life didn't fit in with my plans." She laughed. "Now, he does a lot of traveling."

Kelly didn't want to burst her bubble but felt compelled to remind her. "Long-distance relationships don't usually work."

"No, they don't," Jean agreed. "But I could go with him."

Kelly sagged back in her chair. "And leave everything? The magazine?"

"I might sell it." She glanced around the office for a second as if surveying it. "The buyer I've talked to guaranteed he'd keep my employees. He was especially interested in keeping the writing staff, so you wouldn't—"

Kelly stopped her. "I'm not concerned about that." Uncertainty for her aunt made her question. "What will you do if you sell it?"

"Well, I can't imagine myself playing housewife. Even my meat loaf is terrible," she said lightly, drawing a slim smile from Kelly. "But why can't I have the best of both worlds?"

Is that possible? Kelly wondered.

"You know, Kelly, I agreed with your grandparents when they wanted to stop your mother from leaving with Ray. But later, years later," she said with a reflective look, "I almost envied her."

Kelly's head snapped up. *Envied?* How could her aunt have envied her mother? Jean had had so much more, a successful career, money, famous friends, a lovely penthouse apartment and a life-style that had allowed her to flit off to Europe if she wanted to.

"I knew your mother had a man who loved her." She squeezed Kelly's hand gently and gave her head a small shake. "I never thought I'd have that. Until now."

Kelly understood what her aunt was trying to say, but wasn't her aunt allowing emotion to run her life? "You chose a more exciting life."

She nodded. "I thought I had. But now I want a different kind of excitement. I've done everything I wanted to do, but something was missing. Now, I know what it was. Love," she said softly. "Laughter." She paused for a moment with a reflective look. "When your mother and I were growing up, there wasn't a lot of laughter in our lives. It seemed that when your mother married your father, she was so happy. Then she lost him." A sadness slipped over her face. "Your grandfather took control again then."

As if recalling another time, Jean stared thoughtfully out the window. "I never had the courage to go against his wishes, but your mother did after she met Ray. She was always more independent, more her own person than me."

Kelly felt muddled. "She was?"

Jean laughed softly. "Oh, yes." She tipped her head curiously. "Did you think I was?"

Kelly couldn't deny it. "Yes."

"Oh, no, not me. I always did what I was told. It wasn't until years later after your grandparents were gone that I finally started standing on my own." She smiled wide. "And now, I've decided that I don't want to be alone anymore."

"But you'll be giving up so much."

Her eyes warmer, softer, Jean reached forward and touched Kelly's hand. "Think how much I'll get," she said quietly.

Though she'd never been a solitary person, Kelly had thought that to be her own person, she had to be alone. Yet, here was her aunt, the role model of independence, willingly searching to share her life with someone.

"Be happy for me."

Kelly pushed out of her chair and rounded the desk. "I am." She hugged her aunt. "I really am," she said honestly.

"I'll make sure you meet him soon." Love warmed her voice. "He's always been a very special person to me."

Kelly knew someone like that, too.

Alone minutes later and still confused, she frowned at the ringing telephone and snatched up the receiver quickly. As she heard her realtor's voice, she realized how much she'd hoped she'd hear Denver's.

"It's good you came back when you did," Jeff Culbertson announced. "I don't know how much longer your house will stay on the market now that the seller has lowered the price."

Your house, he'd said. How long had she yearned to have a home of her own? A young girl's dream was finally coming true. She shouldn't be unhappy anymore. This was the moment she'd been waiting for. She set down the receiver, too aware she felt like crying.

There were half a dozen jobs Denver could be doing. He chose the ones that gave him the most solitude. He didn't feel like cracking jokes with the ranch hands or making small talk.

He sat on a stump near his parked truck, and with disinterest, he glanced at the dilapidated fence twenty feet from him. Some crazy notion had made him believe she'd call and tell him she'd made a mistake. That wasn't going to happen.

Nudging himself, he stood, then splashed through the nearby stream to the fallen fence wires. With gloved hands, he yanked the ends of fencing taut, jammed the ends into metal sleeves and pinched them with a pliers. For the next hour, he drifted along the stream, repairing the fence. A squirrel scooted by and up a tree, chattering at his invasion of its territory. Sunlight beat at the back of his neck with a warmth that promised good grazing fields. Routines were part of his life again. Everything was the same as before. Only he was different.

Because of her special caring, bitter emotions that had haunted his adolescence no longer tormented him. Because of her, he'd learned to trust. He should have felt cleansed of pain. Instead, it lingered, gnawing at him, and he knew there was no way to heal it.

By the time he drove back to the ranch, a noon sun shone with glaring brightness down on the backyard and the white tents for the wedding.

He wasn't in the mood for company. Hell, he wasn't in the mood for anything. Sweat rolling down his face, he brushed his sleeve across his forehead. Tired. He was so damn tired, he realized, stopping by the well and dipping a cup into the bucket.

Looking up, he watched his father's lumbering gait. "Folks will be arriving in a few hours."

Denver swallowed the water and remained silent, then dropped the cup into the bucket.

"You're a fool. Go get her. Tell her you love her. You do, don't you?"

Denver shot him a puzzled look.

Will shrugged his shoulders as if shedding off an uncomfortable burden. "I know that I acted differently. But during the fire in the barn, I could see she wasn't like your mother. The ranch and my way of life had never suited her, but Kelly is no city slicker, afraid to break a fingernail."

Denver felt his heart growing heavier. "I know." He'd seen everything his father had, but he also knew he couldn't make Kelly love the life he led. No matter how much he loved her, she had to want this life as much as he did.

He glanced toward the flower truck arriving for the wedding. For Dooley's sake, he had to shove aside his personal turmoil. "She says this isn't her world," he said, stepping away.

He ambled into the den and cursed softly. He couldn't even free himself of her in it. Her neat precise handwriting marked pages in the tally book, her scent clung to the air where she'd worked for hours. She'd made her mark on him and the ranch as surely as if she'd branded everything. They were hers. Only she didn't realize it.

Mr. Culbertson did most of the talking to the sellers. Other than a hello, Kelly remained silent. While he charmed them with an anecdote about his grandson, Kelly strolled into the kitchen. Outside the bay window was a perfect place for a flower garden. During previous visits to the house, she'd contemplated waking on a spring morning and sitting with her coffee cup on the small patio and absorbing the fragrances of the blooms.

But would she have time to nurture that garden? And wouldn't the huge willow block out the sun too much? She whirled away from the window and scanned the kitchen and the hallway. She really didn't like the way the hallway jutted toward one bedroom. And the living room was really too big. The whole house was too big for one person. It was a house meant to shelter a family, to let their laughter echo off its walls.

"Another few minutes," her realtor promised, "and what you've wanted will be yours."

Was that true? She was a signature away from having her dream home and was suddenly feeling nothing. Emotions weren't leading her now. She'd thought long and hard about her future. She'd come back to settle in to what was familiar, to pursue her career. And it wasn't enough.

It had taken her aunt twenty years to learn something was missing. Kelly had always prided herself on being a quicker study. She'd harbored bitter recollections of country living that really had nothing to do with where she'd lived: without her mother, laughter had died. No place had felt like home. Good memories had faded. She'd missed the love of family that she'd once known. It wasn't until she and Jamie had begun living with their aunt that Kelly had recaptured that feeling again.

At some moment to explain away her grief and pain after losing her mother, she'd looked for something to blame for the loss. And she'd been determined not to follow any man's footsteps, believing she'd give up too much. She'd thought avoiding love was the only way to protect herself. But from what? Her mother had loved without regrets. She'd had all she'd wanted, all that was really important.

"Ms. Shelton?" Mr. Culbertson's forehead wrinkled. "I'm having a slight problem. The wife is having second thoughts. That happens often. People raise a family in a house, and when it's time to sell it, all the memories float back at them. Give me another few minutes of negotiating and this could be your home."

No. It would be her house but not her home. She gave her head a disbelieving shake. "Mr. Culbertson, I need to talk to you," she said, stopping him from stepping away to talk to the sellers.

Somehow, she avoided a speeding ticket during the two-hour drive. She arrived in time to see the bride and groom kiss under a flowered trellis at the back of the house in the midst of a blossoming garden. The bride was wearing a high-necked, lacy Victorian dress. The groom wore a Western suit and his boots. Around her, dressed in their Sunday finery, neighbors circled the couple.

Lingering back, she watched the finalizing of two people pledging themselves to each other. Not all their moments would be good, but neither of them would ever stand alone again.

"I told Charlie you'd come," Lorna said, and swept Kelly into her arms for a hug.

Kelly held on tight for a long moment, trying to draw courage from this woman's strength.

Pulling back, Lorna winked. "I'll tell Denver you're here."

"No, wait." Kelly grabbed her arm.

Lorna raised a questioning eyebrow.

"Don't say anything yet," Kelly appealed.

"I don't think I'll have to." Lorna motioned with her head toward the wedding guests wandering off in different directions, some heading for the food table, others more interested in the country band tuning up their instruments.

Wending his way through them, Denver stopped abruptly. Though his eyes locked with hers, he offered no smile, no acknowledgement. She felt doubts surging forward.

Affectionately Will passed by and touched her shoulder. "I'm glad you came."

Kelly returned his smile as her stomach fluttered with nerves. She watched Denver's gaze sweep over her peach-colored suit. It wasn't really appropriate, but she'd decided that he hadn't played fair before. This time it was her turn. "Dooley invited me," she said when he was inches from her.

Touch her, hold her. The thoughts flooded his mind, but he wasn't a man to self-inflict pain. He'd spilled feelings to her, had come close to begging. Pride demanded more of him now. But he didn't think it was possible to yearn more for her. "I knew he would." She looked so damn beautiful to him. It was a thought Denver shied away from. "Have a good time."

She couldn't say what she'd expected him to say. She heard no warmth, no softness in his voice. Stunned as he whipped around to step away, Kelly snagged his arm. "Wait."

He swung back, determined to harden his heart. He wasn't a good loser, he realized. He wanted it all with her, not a stolen moment or two when she was in the mood. He'd waited too many years, had thought he might never find a woman to erase the hurt his mother had inflicted. He needed a woman who'd share his life with him. "I'm not interested in some part-time romance."

The breath she was drawing stuck in her throat. A rehearsed speech fled from her mind. She glanced away, ready to run before she burst into tears and made more of a fool of herself. Stubbornly she rooted her feet. She couldn't leave. A lifetime of happiness depended on her showing some courage. "I didn't come for that."

She noticed stares. She didn't care that they'd drawn an audience. This moment might be her last with him. "I don't want that, either." She let out a shaky breath. If only he'd step closer, open his arms to her. "I packed everything I own and drove here. I'm not afraid to admit that I made a mistake, that I want more with you than . . ." She paused as his eyes softened with a look of disbelief.

Amazingly Denver somehow kept from yanking her close. Once she was in his arms, he knew he'd never let her go. "What about your work?"

The beginnings of annoyance were taking control. She would not, she absolutely would not beg him. But if he didn't hold her pretty soon, she was going to throw herself at him. "I have that all worked out. I might have to commute sometimes for interviews, but I'll do free-lance writing. And I could always do some writing for the local newspaper."

He wanted to take everything she'd just said and not question it, not allow himself to think beyond the moment. But he'd gone through hell once. He wouldn't go through it again. If she stayed, he had to know it was for keeps. Deliberately he waited and drew a steadying breath. "I witnessed firsthand what happens when someone is forced into a life they don't want. What about your life in the city?"

She couldn't believe they were having such a sensible conversation. "This isn't Antarctica." She attempted a smile, hoping for a similar response. "I can visit."

"What did your aunt say about this?"

At the moment, the last thing she wanted to do was explain everything. "I'll go to the city with you and visit my aunt and my sister. Anyway, my aunt isn't too sure that she'll be keeping her magazine," she said quickly, to keep conversation going, afraid he'd walk away if she didn't. "She might be getting married."

Denver stared quizzically at her.

"I know. I'm surprised, too. But she's found someone she's always wanted. Me, too," she added softly.

His eyebrows knit. "You, too?" he asked, uncertain he'd heard her correctly. "I'm not quite clear on everything." He tilted his head in the manner of someone with a hearing problem. "Did you just propose to me?"

She began to relax, began to warm inside with the rightness of her actions. "Well, you're so slow, I thought I'd better do it or—" She stopped with a laugh as he yanked her into his arms.

A smile tugged at his lips. "You sure? Are you absolutely sure?" he insisted on knowing, but the arms around her were unyielding.

"Absolutely." She raised her face to his and touched a fingertip to his lips. "It didn't take long for me to realize that you're more important than anything else."

He grabbed her hand and drew her away from the curious crowd and around to the side of the house. With a hard fierce kiss, his mouth closed over hers. Long and deep, the kiss carried a message that bound them together.

Through misty eyes, she met his gaze. "It's so hard to explain. But memories from my past, not of the country, but of the sadness I felt after my mother died, got all tangled together. I thought she'd given up everything important." She brushed her lips across his. "I didn't remember that no matter where she was, she'd always been happy, always had love with her."

He tightened his hold on her. "Give me more."

Give him. Yes, she wanted to give because she knew now what love was. It was a lot of give and take. Mostly it was about sharing. "I want to be with you wherever you are," she said softly. "I love you. I don't even know when it started." With a laugh, she leaned into him. "Maybe when you sat in the restaurant with your legs stretched out under that small table." She tightened her arms on his back. "I only know it will never go away. Not ever."

Denver framed her face with his hands. "You wore that damn peach-colored suit deliberately, didn't you?"

She traced the curve of a dimple. "You bet."

Brushing strands of hair away from her cheek, he needed to hear one more thing from her. "This is your choice. It has to be."

Around them, she heard the buzz of conversation. No one else mattered. "Aren't you listening? You're my choice," she whispered against his mouth.

* * * * *

**And now for
something completely different
from Silhouette....**

Unique and innovative stories that take you into the world of paranormal happenings. Look for our special "Spellbound" flash—and get ready for a truly exciting reading experience!

**In February, look for
One Unbelievable Man (SR #993)
by Pat Montana.**

Was he man or myth? Cass Kohlmann's mysterious traveling companion, Michael O'Shea, had her all confused. He'd suddenly appeared, claiming she was his destiny—determined to win her heart. But could levelheaded Cass learn to believe in fairy tales...before her fantasy man disappeared forever?

Don't miss the charming, sexy and utterly mysterious
Michael O'Shea in
ONE UNBELIEVABLE MAN.
Watch for him in February—only from

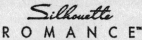

R O M A N C E™

SPELL2

**Relive the romance...
Harlequin and Silhouette
are proud to present**

by Request ™

A program of collections of three complete novels by the most requested
authors with the most requested themes. Be sure to look for one volume each
month with three complete novels by top name authors.

In January: **WESTERN LOVING**   Susan Fox
                                      JoAnn Ross
                                      Barbara Kaye

Loving a cowboy is easy—taming him isn't!

In February: **LOVER, COME BACK!**   Diana Palmer
                                      Lisa Jackson
                                      Patricia Gardner Evans

It was over so long ago—yet now they're calling, "Lover, Come Back!"

In March: **TEMPERATURE RISING** JoAnn Ross
                                      Tess Gerritsen
                                      Jacqueline Diamond

Falling in love—just what the doctor ordered!

Available at your favorite retail outlet.

REQ-G3

 HARLEQUIN®  *Silhouette*®

**It's our 1000th
Silhouette Romance
and we're celebrating!**

Join us for a special collection of love stories by the authors you've loved for years, and new favorites you've just discovered.

**It's a celebration just for you,
with wonderful books by
Diana Palmer, Suzanne Carey,
Tracy Sinclair, Marie Ferrarella,
Debbie Macomber, Laurie Paige,
Annette Broadrick, Elizabeth August
and MORE!**

Silhouette Romance...vibrant, fun and emotionally rich! Take another look at us!

As part of the celebration, readers can receive a FREE gift AND enter our exciting sweepstakes to win a grand prize of $1000! Look for more details in all March Silhouette series titles.

**You'll fall in love all over again
with Silhouette Romance!**

Silhouette

SPECIAL EDITION

Nora Roberts

CONVINCING ALEX

Those Wild Ukrainians

Look who Detective Alex Stanislaski has picked up....

When soap opera writer Bess McNee hit the streets in spandex pants and a clinging tube-top in order to research the role of a prostitute, she was looking for trouble—but not too much trouble.

Then she got busted by straight-laced Detective Alex Stanislaski and found a lot more than she'd bargained for. This man wasn't buying anything she said, and Bess realized she was going to have to be a *lot* more convincing....

If you enjoyed TAMING NATASHA (SE #583), LURING A LADY (SE #709) and FALLING FOR RACHEL (SE #810), then be sure to read CONVINCING ALEX, the delightful tale of another one of THOSE WILD UKRAINIANS finding love where it's least expected.

SSENR